Suddenly Supernatural

SCAREDY KAT

by

Elizabeth Cody Kimmel

LITTLE, BROWN AND COMPANY

Books for Young Readers

New York   Boston

For Elizabeth O'Malley
—E.C.K

Little, Brown and Company

Hachette Book Group
237 Park Avenue, New York, NY 10017
Visit our Web site at www.lb-kids.com

First Edition: February 2009

The characters and events portrayed in this book are
fictitious. Any similarity to real persons, living or dead,
is coincidental and not intended by the author.

Library of Congress Cataloging-in-Publication Data

Kimmel, Elizabeth Cody.
    Scaredy Kat / by Elizabeth Cody Kimmel. — 1st ed.
    p. cm. — (Suddenly supernatural)
    Summary: Thirteen-year-old Kat, still not comfortable in her role as a
medium, and her friend Jac, undergoing a serious crisis about the role
of music in her life, try to find a way to help the unhappy spirit of a
young boy in the abandoned house next door.
    ISBN 978-0-316-06685-3
    [1. Spiritualists—Fiction. 2. Supernatural—Fiction. 3.
Friendship—Fiction. 4. Mothers and daughters—Fiction.] I. Title.
    PZ7.K56475Sc 2009
    [Fic]—dc22
                                                    2008005025

6/09

10 9 8 7 6 5 4 3 2 1

RRD-C

Printed in the United States of America

The text was set in RuseX, and the display type is Oneleigh

Chapter 1

The truth is, I find it very embarrassing when my mother talks to plants.

There, I've said it. I can't tell her, you see. She'd feel bad, and that's the last thing I want. In most respects, she's incredibly cool. She's a free spirit who lives her beliefs and doesn't worry about what people think about her. She's fun, and wise, and sponta-neous. But she's also a walkie-talkie to the spirit world, and now, apparently, so am I.

I've kind of made my peace with the fact

that I've started to see dead people. After all, I did grow up in a house with a mom who communicated with the dead as if they were Girl Scouts dropping by to sell cookies. And this sort of thing runs in families, so I wasn't totally stunned when I started seeing ghosts a few months back, the day I turned thirteen.

But I wasn't exactly thrilled about it, either. Given the choice, I'm not sure I would have chosen *medium* as my life path. But you know. Stuff happens, and you figure out how to deal with it. My mom deals.

And that sometimes involves her chatting up flowers.

There weren't any ghosts in Carlson's plant nursery, just tons of luscious, flowering plants in the greenhouse. Mom says it's very easy to attune yourself to the spirits of trees and plants. They are aware of us and have a kind of love for us if we're open to it. And, well, she's open to it. Like, very open.

So we spent the morning strolling through the morning glories and the orange symphonies and the orchids, and my mom was quietly chatting with them, exchanging little pleasantries the way most moms do with other parents at soccer matches. When I was sure no one was looking, I gave it a try, just out of curiosity. I asked a tiger lily how it was doing, but it just sort of . . . sat there.

That's how I spent the first morning of spring break. My best friend, Jac, was away at some kind of conference for young musical geniuses, because she is one. So after my mom and I went to Carlson's, I had to content myself with obsessively checking for her e-mails, and hanging around the garden while my mother raked out the flower beds to prepare them for the new plantings.

"Any word from Jac?" she asked. Her pale blond hair was pulled up in a high ponytail, and she had a smudge of dirt on her cheek, and another on her faded Beatles T-shirt. From a certain angle in the shade, she looked about sixteen.

"No," I sighed as I flopped down on my trampoline, kicking my feet up and down like I was trying to swim.

"Maybe she doesn't have Internet access."

"She brought her laptop to the hotel. Everybody has Internet access. It's all wireless now. Her mother is probably guarding her."

Jac's mother was excessively ambitious about her daughter's musical career. Much more ambitious, actually, than Jac was.

"Did Jac even want to go to this conference?"

Another worm was whisked away to a new home in the soil.

"She did *not* seem happy about it," I replied. "The only thing she was looking forward to was seeing some of her music friends. She says there are some things only another baby music genius can understand."

Just like there were some things only another thirteen-year-old ghost whisperer could understand. Except I didn't know any other teen ghost whisperers.

"Well, she's got a very strong personality, Kat," my mother said, kneeling in the flower bed again. "Hopefully she won't let her mother control her."

"You don't know her mother," I said ruefully. "I'm going to go check my inbox again," I added, rolling up to a sitting position. It was that or fall asleep on the trampoline.

I was momentarily blind after walking inside, out of the bright sunlight. Our house, a somewhat run-down old Victorian, was perpetually dark downstairs. I fumbled up the stairs, regaining my sight in the narrow creaky hallway that led to my room. Sun streamed through the windows onto my bed and across the floor, illuminating the amazing mess.

I sat down at my desk and clicked on my e-mail icon, almost immediately giving a little shout.

"Finally!"

To: Voodoo Mama

From: Maestra

Subject: My So-called Spring Vacation

Yes, I know, SORRY for not e-mailing sooner! My mother is all over me. Things

are not going well at all, but I'll have to give you the details in person. The only good thing I can say is I've been able to hang out with my friend Tee, a violinist. We go way back — seriously, I think we met at some baby genius convention when we were still in Pull-Ups. It's good to have someone to talk to, except my mother is always hovering somewhere nearby, probably to make sure I don't hatch a plot to escape.

Write back, hopefully with more interesting news than I have. Any ghostly activity going on? Levitating chickens, talking statues, that kind of thing? I hope so, because I am *ready* for a little excitement. Peace,

Jac

For a girl who had a conniption fit every time she saw a bug, Jac was certainly fearless in the paranormal department. But I had nothing more interesting to tell her than the fact that my mom had been making friends with worms. So far, spring break was a bust for Jac and me both.

I stared out my window. Below, I could see my mother's form bent over the garden. Beyond the trampoline was a low wall separating our yard from the house next door. An old Victorian like ours, it had been empty ever since we moved in two years ago.

Down the street, there were two construction vans parked outside. One of them said DIGNUM CONTRACTORS on the side. This *could* mean the house had been sold, and the new owner was fixing it up. Maybe some nice family would move in, paint the place, and spice up our end of the block a little. I imagined an easygoing, friendly couple with little children, or maybe even a girl close to my age.

They'd have a barbecue outside and would grill burgers on nice evenings. I'd invite their kids over to jump on the trampoline. We'd call friendly little greetings to each other from our yards.

Or. They'd overhear my mother talking to plants and worms, and from that day forward they'd rush into the house and pull the blinds whenever they caught sight of us.

I sighed and went back to my desk. I read Jac's e-mail again, then hit REPLY.

To: Maestra
From: Voodoo Mama

SO RELIEVED to hear from you! Was starting to worry you had been taken captive by the menacing cello cult. You're supposed to be back in two days, right? Boredom here is excruciating. Only thing going

on is workmen showed up at abandoned house next door, so possibility of new neighbors exists. Good thing? Bad thing? You decide.

Take care of you. Sneak away with Tee or something. Have a little fun! What can your maternal unit do, really? You're practically grounded already, anyway.

Have you started your basic communications project yet? I haven't. Don't let me leave it 'til the last day . . .

Get home already. And write back.

Peace,

Kat

I stared at the e-mail for a moment. It seemed stupid when I read it. It didn't sound like me, and didn't communicate what I really wanted to say. I wasn't one of those girls who was good at instant messaging and texting. Not that I had a group of people to IM or text *to*. Can't talk to plants like my mom can, can't IM like most of the civilized world can. Sometimes I suspected I didn't fit in *anywhere.*

My eye rested on the line about the basic communications project. BC was essentially seventh grade English class with a fancier name and occasional forays into creative projects like this one. We were assigned to tell a story using two forms — written word and a second of our choice. I had picked photography because it seemed easy, I had a new digital camera I had gotten for Christmas that I hadn't figured out how to use yet, and I liked the idea of capturing things on film.

But what was I supposed to write about and take pictures of? I hit SEND on the e-mail, then got up and walked to the window. It looked like the workmen were packing up and calling it a day. I watched them stowing their gear in the vans, then fixed my gaze on the empty windows next door, which stared back at me like eyes. I should just do the project on the house, I thought. It's the only vaguely interesting thing around.

I could tell its story in words, imagining the people who had lived there in the last century and where they had gone. And I could tell the story in photographs, using different angles and light to give the house different moods. Really, as vacation assignments went, this one might not be so bad.

I got my camera out of my desk drawer and turned on the power. It was a good camera, probably more than my mother could really have afforded. I opened my window and framed the two second-floor windows, twins to my own. I snapped a few shots, tinkering with the adjustments. I was still getting used to the way the camera worked, and I had never tried uploading shots to my computer.

I popped the little Smart Card out of the camera and into the media slot in my computer. Happily, the uploading process began by itself. Good. This was going to be easy to get the hang of.

I clicked on my new picture file, and there were thumbnails of the three shots I'd taken. I opened the first one and examined it. It was a dud, too off-center and with part of my window frame messing up the focus. The second one had my window frame in it, too. I clicked on the third picture. Much better.

It was a clear shot of both windows. The

sun had gone behind a cloud, so there was no glare on the glass, except for an oval smudge in the center of one pane. What was that? I enlarged and enhanced the section of the picture with the smudge and examined it.

It was the pale face of a little boy, looking directly into the camera.

Chapter 2

I pored over the image, enlarging it as much as possible on my computer, but it was impossible to make much out. It was definitely a boy's face, I was sure of that. He had dark hair and might have been around nine or ten years old. Beyond that, I couldn't see much.

The thing is, when I returned to my window and looked out, there was nothing there. And I had seen nothing through the view-finder. I was still way too new at this spirit world ambassador gig to know what this meant, or what I was supposed to do, if anything. I had really only acted as a medium once before, a few months back at school when I had helped the spirit of a student who had died in the sixties. She had been haunting the old music room, which was now the library. But that spirit had basically sought me out, or as it turns out, sought Jac and me out together. Though it hadn't seemed so at the time, the experience was kind of like uploading photos from my camera. I was helped along, step by step. But a face appearing on a photographic image when I could not see one with my own eyes, this was new territory.

I decided the next logical step would be to take more photographs of the house, to see if the face popped up again. I shot a few pictures from my window again, then walked to my mother's bedroom. The large bay window there faced the part of the old house closest to the street, giving me a slightly different angle. Then I went downstairs and outside, where I took pictures of the front of the house. I was about to cross the street to get some wide angle shots, when I noticed a tall, kind of cute man standing across the street next to a bicycle that was leaning up against a signpost. Because he was looking at the house kind of intently, I figured he must be one of the workmen. But there was no Dignum Contractors van, or any vehicle, in sight. So maybe he was the guy who had bought the house.

I ducked back through our front door, then in full junior spy mode I peeked through the window to get a better look at my possible future neighbor. Using the camera's zoom lens as makeshift binoculars, I was able to inspect him more closely. He had the kind of face that didn't give away his age — I guessed maybe he was in his forties, but he could have been younger or older. He had shaggy black hair with gray mixed in — what my mom called a salt-and-pepper look. His forehead was creased with lines, and his eyebrows furrowed as he stared at the house like he was looking for something.

Weird. I watched him through the viewfinder until I started to feel uncomfortably like a stalker. Almost without thinking, I pressed the shutter button and snapped his photograph before lowering the camera. If he *was* in fact our new neighbor, I wasn't sure how I felt about it. He didn't look like the type to barbecue in the backyard. He looked way too intense for that. But I guess you never know. Anyway, for all I knew he was some kind of architect or birdwatcher or simply your run of the mill nutjob.

Comforting.

I finished up out back in our yard, where my mother was still conducting her earthworm convention. She had also planted half the orange symphonies, and I listened to her humming to herself as I captured a final few images of the house, then climbed onto my trampoline to lounge.

"Figured it out yet?" my mother asked me, standing back to admire the flowers while brushing dirt from her jeans.

At first I thought she meant the face in the window, which kind of freaked me out. Of all the psychic abilities my mother possessed, thankfully mind reading had never been on the list. Then I realized with relief that she was referring to the camera. Nobody wants a mind-reading mom. Nobody.

"Yeah, pretty much," I said, crawling out the little opening in the trampoline's netted safety enclosure and hopping down onto the grass. "I got the upload thingy to work, so I can finally get pictures onto the computer. And I've been playing with the zoom lens and everything. It's a great camera. I'm going to use it for my basic communications project."

"Really? You picked a topic?"

I nodded, and gestured toward the old house.

"I'm going to tell the story of that house in words and photographs," I explained.

My mother looked across the fence at the house. She was silent for a few moments, her eyes half closed.

"Mmm," she said. "Yeah. You should come up with some great stuff there."

I wasn't sure if that meant she had sensed something, and I didn't ask. I didn't want to get into the habit of running to my mom every time I saw a spirit. Since it was apparently going to be happening on a very regular basis, I needed to start working on developing my own instincts.

"Well, I'm going to go take a shower," she said, giving me a smile. "I feel like a potato that's just been dug up."

I held up the camera.

"I'm going to go to my room and upload these," I said. "Might as well get schoolwork done while Jac's still away."

"Oh, Kat, I'm sorry," my mom said. "You don't have much to distract you, what with me in the garden and Jac away. Not much of a vacation. I should have planned something for us to do."

"It's okay," I said. "I'm actually kind of enjoying this photography thing."

She gave me one of her intent looks, like she was trying to figure something out.

"Good," she said, brushing my hair out of my eyes. Then she walked up the little brick path that led to our back door. Before going inside, I noticed her glance up at the house next door.

It made me wonder. Had she seen the face, too?

Before taking the memory card from my camera, I took one last picture — this one was of me with my tongue out. I'd send it to Jac, for a laugh.

The pictures obediently appeared on my screen in miniature form, one after the other. I clicked through them, one at a time. Nothing. The photographs were interesting in their own way, but the phantom face didn't appear in any of them, at least not that I could see. I sat back in my chair, arms folded, and scowled at the screen. Why would the boy show up in just one picture? I clicked on the e-mail icon so that I wouldn't have to keep looking at the little images lined up on the screen like tiny Tarot cards. I e-mailed my tongue-sticking-out picture to Jac without examining it closely — I didn't really need to know all the facial imperfections my high-tech digital camera could pick up.

At that point, I should have just let the issue of the boy's face go. The ghost at school had come to me — had worked to get my attention. This one was playing hard to get. Maybe it had been a mistake. Maybe my camera had captured him unaware. It shouldn't matter. I was coming to know that the world was full of ghosts, every hallway and staircase a potential portal to another

dimension. I had chanced upon a face looking out of the window of an empty house.
Now it was gone. I should just leave it at
that.

But I couldn't.

I could hear the shower running. I walked
down the hall to the bathroom, opened the
door a crack, and called that I was going out
for a little walk. A technical truth.

I went downstairs and into the living
room to retrieve my shoes. From his doggie
bed, Max, my German Shepherd, raised his
head and stared at me with huge brown
eyes. His expression seemed concerned and
slightly disapproving.

"Don't look at me that way," I said to
him. "It's no big deal."

Max gave a knowing, weary sigh, and
lowered his head back onto his paws. He

continued to watch me as I laced my sneakers. In a house where people could see the dead, get messages from the underworld, and commune with plant life, it didn't seem all that strange that Max seemed to know what I was about to do. Psychic German Shepherd. It would make a great reality show. Or a very good reason to lock me up in the nuthouse.

I walked out of the living room without looking back at Max. I felt guilty enough about not being entirely truthful with my mother — I didn't need Max's Disney Eyes making me feel even worse. Anyway, I wasn't really going to do anything all that wrong. I was working on a school project. There was no one living in the house. I was just going over to get some closer shots. It was all innocent enough.

And if a door or window happened to be unlocked, what was the harm in having one little peek inside?

Our backyard was separated from the yard next door by an old stone wall that I easily climbed over; my camera hung around my neck. Standing there, it was like I'd tumbled into another world. Nothing had been touched in this yard for several years. The grass came to my waist, and vines had crept up an old swing set and twined around its poles as if they intended to swallow it whole. The paint on the house was peeling off in large chunks, and the steps to the screened-in porch looked like they might be rotted. Our house and garden looked strange from this viewpoint — it was like peering back through the wardrobe from

Narnia and catching a glimpse of the room back home.

I was making my way carefully through the tangle of plant growth toward the back porch when my foot connected with something. I reached down and felt for it with my hand, my fingers touching something small and metal. I picked it up. It was a little armored vehicle, about the size of an old Hot Wheels car, army green with a white star. I turned it over in my hands, then without really thinking about it, I stuck it in my sweatshirt pocket.

The steps leading to the porch were much more solid than they looked. The porch door was locked, but since the screen already had a huge hole in it, I just reached through and unlocked the door from the inside. There was nothing on the porch itself, except for an old set of wind chimes hanging from above. They were tangled, and I reached up and unknotted them so they would swing free again. I've always loved the sound of wind chimes.

The door from the porch into the house was locked, but a window on the same wall was open. It was a much bigger leap of faith to climb through the window than it had been to unlatch the broken screen door, but something within me was determined to get inside the house. I threw one leg over the windowsill, ducked my head, and hoisted myself through.

I was standing in a kitchen. The air smelled stale and a little sour, but unlike the outside of the house, the kitchen was in pretty good shape and neat as a pin other than some dust and cobwebs. The wooden cupboards and shelves were painted a cheerful avocado green, and the linoleum floor was scrubbed clean. A small table and two chairs were the only furniture there. On the other side of the kitchen, I could see another room, and a narrow hallway beyond it. I crossed the kitchen and went through the doorway.

Probably the dining room, I thought. Like the kitchen, it was dusty but otherwise neat and in perfect condition. The hardwood floors were smooth and creaked slightly under my feet. The sun shone in windowpane squares across the floral wallpaper. I was suddenly enveloped by the smell of baking bread, as strong as if I had just walked into the local pastry shop. I turned and looked back toward the empty kitchen, which looked bright and inviting in the late afternoon sun. Strange. The house looked so rundown and creepy on the outside. But from inside, it was perfect.

The aroma of bread now powerfully scented the air, and though it was a comforting and familiar smell, my heart started beating harder. I had never picked up a ghost smell before.

The hallway passed a stairway to the right and led to the front door. At the end of the hall were rooms to the left and the right, and there was another little doorway under the stairs. It reminded me of the closet Harry Potter lived in at the Dursleys. I opened the door and peered inside to find a little, neatly appointed bathroom.

I reached the end of the hall, and turned through the door on the left, into a sitting room. I barely had time to register the fact that there was a fire burning in the fireplace when the sound of a piercing scream froze me in my tracks.

Chapter 3

I instinctively whirled around to look behind me, though the scream had come from inside the sitting room. When I turned back, the ghost fire was gone and the fireplace dark.

I waited, cautiously, to see if anything else was going to happen. This medium business could leave a person's nerves totally shot. Sometimes I felt like I was in one of those suspense movies where the audience can always see who's creeping up, but the person in the movie is totally oblivious. At least in the movies the music gets all weird when something unexpected is about to happen. I could use a soundtrack of my own. Standing in the silence waiting for a noise or a smell or a glimpse of something was making me absolutely nuts.

Another scream rang through the air, but now that I was listening so closely, it sounded more like a playful scream. Like somebody was being tickled or something. I relaxed slightly, until my eye caught movement from the corner of the room. A small ball was rolling toward me. It stopped precisely at my feet. Maybe it was an invitation to play, but I had no intention of accepting it. I took a picture of the room, and another one of the ball. Then I heard footsteps overhead. Was there no end to the supernatural activity in this house?

Someone was up there. Not a little boy, but someone much heavier. A man, maybe.

Alive? Or not? There was absolutely no way for me to know. I went to the bottom of the stairs and tried the front door. It was locked. I heard a thud from upstairs, and my heart began thumping in my chest. I couldn't stand that I was so afraid, and that I couldn't control those feelings. What was the point, I wondered for the hundredth time, of being gifted with spirit sight when half of the time the very glimpse of a ghost freaked me out half to death? I hated that about myself. It was like being a fisherman who was afraid of the water, or a weatherman afraid of lightning.

And if I fled the house now, that would only make it worse. I took a deep breath and started up the staircase, clutching the banister a lot more tightly than I needed to. The stairs led to a rectangular landing with three doors. The sound had come from the room at the front of the house, facing the street. I tried to focus on something cheerful as I walked down the hall, and settled on an image of Max's face. My mother had said something once about certain types of spirits who could sense fear and drew their energy from it. I didn't want to be the Red Bull fueling some crazy spirit with a surge of power.

The door to the front bedroom stood open, and I walked inside. I could see part of my house through one of the windows. The glimpse of home made me feel a little more comfortable. I took a shaky breath, closed my eyes, and opened my mind. It's difficult to explain what that means. It's not like there's some Internet chat room where psychic people hang out and discuss these things. Actually, there probably is, but I haven't stumbled upon it yet. I don't know what other mediums do to establish contact with a spirit. I'm not even sure exactly what it is that *I* do. I start by sort of visualizing myself as a giant satellite dish scanning the sky for a radio signal. I think I took the idea from images of the Very Large Array in New Mexico, where dozens of these huge antennae are pointed out into the galaxy to search for signs of astronomical events.

I wasn't picking up anything I could identify, but I had a growing sense of unease. And suddenly I knew I was not alone. I opened my eyes and looked around cautiously. A voice in my head told me to turn around. The feeling in my stomach told me not to. My heart pounded so hard I felt faint. Wasn't anything better than standing here hyperventilating?

I whirled around.

And shrieked.

He was standing so close behind me we

were practically touching. I took a step back, pressing one hand to my chest. The man was very old, but still cut a towering figure. His shoulders were bent but broad, and his neck was thick and muscled. His face was deeply creased and lined, and his hair pure white. But what paralyzed me were those ice-blue eyes fixed intently on mine, and absolutely glittering with hatred.

"You," he hissed at me.

I gulped, speechless.

"A Living One who sees the dead," he said. "You." Then he raised a finger and jabbed the air, pointing at me. His image rippled.

I shook my head and took another step away from him. It was wrong to show fear, wrong to feel it. This was an earthbound spirit. I was a medium. I could help him, if he wanted it. It's what I was supposed to do.

It's what my mother would do without question. But there was incredible anger coming off of this spirit. I didn't want to have anything to do with it. Plainly put, I was scared of him.

I didn't offer.

"See me," the man said.

Was it a command? A question?

He took a step forward, finger jabbing in the air again.

"See me!" he shouted.

Almost as a reflex, I stuck the camera between us, and pushed the button. The white blue light of the flash bathed the room and just as instantly disappeared.

So did the old man.

I hightailed it out of the room, slamming the door behind me.

I ran to the top of the stairs, then paused.

The door I had closed remained shut.

Nothing came through it. The angry old man was not coming after me. And I suspected that if I opened that door and looked back into the room, I would find him gone.

But I didn't look.

I was pathetic. Kat, the scaredy-cat medium.

I'd only felt this scared once before, when I had gone to the library at dawn looking for the troubled spirit of Suzanne Bennis. I had found her, but there had been something else there, too, something dark and menacing. A powerful malevolent force that I knew had never been human. That dark shadow had scared me; I knew one day I'd have to face it again. I still dreamed of it from time to time. The old man wasn't like that dark shadow — his was the energy of a human soul, however tormented. But his rage chilled me to the bone.

The sun had dipped below the horizon, and the house was growing darker. I wanted to go home. But the image of the little boy gnawed at me. I had come into the house to find him. I was trespassing on private property, and on the territory of the dead. Having done all that, could I go home now without checking the boy's room — the one that faced my own bedroom? I had accepted the fact that I was always going to see dead people, like it or not. I had to make peace with it. Was I going to let this house run me off?

I turned and faced the second door — the room next to the old man's. The room whose windows looked directly into my bedroom. *There must be a reason,* I told myself. *Something to explain why I feel so compelled to find this boy. If he needs me so much, he won't try to frighten me, or hurt me.*

Would he?

I felt light-headed, and a little nause-ated. I took a deep breath and walked quickly into the room. The first thing I noticed was something painted on the wall — not graf-fiti or something a child had done. A real artist had painted this. It was a sunburst painted in ripples of green, purple, and gold, maybe four feet across. I instantly loved it, and found it hard to take my eyes off the painting. I was happy just to stand there and take it in.

Until I felt a new presence.

He was sitting on the floor under the window, playing with something that could have been marbles or toy soldiers. He looked about ten years old, with soot-colored hair that hung in his eyes. He was humming something to himself — a tune I recognized but could not place.

"Hi there," I said.

The boy didn't look up or indicate that he'd heard me at all. He just kept playing and humming.

"My name's Kat," I continued. "I live in the house next door."

Nothing.

"I can see your windows from my room."

Nothing.

"What are you playing?"

I was beginning to feel stupid, the way you would if you were talking to a real live kid who was ignoring your every word. But there was something about this boy, something about his energy, that made me want to protect him. From what, I had no idea.

"Is this your room?" I asked, taking a few steps closer to him.

Again, he didn't respond, but he abruptly stopped humming and looked up. Not at me, but at something else. It was almost as if something on the ceiling had caught his attention. Then I did hear him say something, but it was so soft I couldn't make it out.

"What did you say?" I asked.

His lips kept moving as he gazed up, his head tilted back so that his bangs no longer hid his eyes.

"I'm here," the boy whispered to the ceiling.

I took another step forward, faster than I meant to move.

"I know that," I said, a little eagerly. "I can see you. Can't you see me?"

"I'm here," the boy repeated. "I'm here."

He wasn't talking to me. He hadn't looked in my direction. Unlike Suzanne Bennis from the school library, or the old man in the next room, this spirit didn't seem to know I was there listening to him. Seeing him.

"I don't understand," I said. "Can you hear me? My name is Kat."

Still, he didn't look at me. I was so close to him right now I could see that his eyes, which were a startling hazel, were filling with tears.

"I'm in here," the boy whispered.

What was I supposed to do? Spirits saw me. They always saw me. But this one, whom I had broken into a house to find, could not or would not acknowledge I was there.

"Please," I said to him, kneeling down so that my face was level with his. "Can't you just turn your head and look? Or nod if you understand me?"

He just kept looking up at that one spot. Like he was talking to God or something. Like someone was standing over him, looking down at him.

"No, don't," he began.

And just like that, I was alone.

I put my hand out and lightly touched the place on the floor where he'd been sitting. It was stone cold. The sun was setting, its rays shining orange and rose through the window and illuminating the painting with warm light. From where I was still kneeling, I could see that something was written under the painting. Moving closer to the wall, I could make it out clearly. *For Tank. Let your light shine. Love, Aunt Ruby.* A date was written underneath. Three years ago, about ten months before we'd moved next door. I took a picture of the painting.

Something told me that Tank was the little boy's name, or maybe I was just so desperate to know something about him I'd decided the painting and inscription were for him. So now I knew where he lived, what he looked like, and what his name was, or at least what I intended to call him. That was more than I found out about most spirits in the first encounter. What, then, was stopping him from communicating directly with me? He was old enough to talk.

This is stupid, I told myself. You've seen him. You've tried to make yourself known to him. There's nothing else to do here.

The sun had now dropped down below the horizon. The house felt cold and dark. I thought of the old man in the next room and suppressed a shiver at the memory of his rage. It was definitely time to get out of there.

But before I left, I walked over to Tank's window, where I'd first seen him. I'd left my computer on in my room, and I could see the blue rectangle of its screen perfectly. The lights in the kitchen were on — my mother was probably starting dinner. My stomach rumbled. I was about to turn to go, when something caught my eye. There was a light covering of dust on the windowpanes, and something had been traced over it with a finger. I leaned closer so that I could make out the words.

The backwards letters spelled: HELP ME.

Chapter 4

"I'm back! Going upstairs for a while, 'kay?"
I called over my shoulder to my mom, all
while practically sprinting for the stairs. If I
had to come face-to-face with her at this moment, she would know there was something
wrong. And I didn't want to talk about it. Not
now. Not with her. Why? I wasn't sure. I suspected it had something to do with the fear I
could still feel in the pit of my stomach. I
kept seeing that old man's face in my mind's
eye. Mediums weren't supposed to be fearful.
I didn't want my mother to know how weak I

was. And I didn't want a lecture about how there was nothing to fear but fear itself.

"Sure, Kat, we can eat whenever you're ready," I heard her say.

I wasn't sure I'd ever be ready for food that night. I still felt light-headed, and now my stomach was a little upset to boot. When I got to my room, the first thing I did was pull my curtains closed. They were light and flimsy, and the sun shone right through them in the mornings, but closing them gave me the illusion that whatever was in the house next door wouldn't be able to see me. I put on a Norah Jones CD. The music was relaxing. I lay on my bed for a few minutes, listening and taking long deep breaths. I still didn't feel quite myself, but my stomach did feel a bit better.

After a while, I felt so safe and comfortable in my room that I began to wonder if

I'd overreacted to the house. It wasn't like I hadn't expected the place to be haunted. When a house has been around for a hundred and fifty years, it would be weird to not find any ghosts there. Nothing truly bad had happened. I'd just gotten a little startled. The more I thought about it, the better I felt.

I got up and plugged the camera's memory card into my computer. I examined each picture as it came up. The shots I'd taken outside the house showed nothing out of the ordinary. When I came to the shot of Tank's room, I drew my breath in sharply. I recognized the walls and window of the room, but obscuring the painting was a ball-shaped sphere of light suspended in the air.

A spirit orb.

I had only read about and seen pictures of them, but I knew one when I saw it. Spirit orbs were supposed to contain the soul and life experience of a dead person. I couldn't remember much more about them. So I Googled the term, and got a hit on a site I'd visited before called spiritworldcenter.com. The site explained:

An orb may represent a single spirit, or it may be a community of souls. Orbs can be as small as ping pong balls or as large as watermelons. They are frequently observed shooting through rooms and pass easily through solid material, though some orbs are known to hover around certain humans, for reasons that remain unknown.

What the site didn't explain was how I could catch a spirit orb with my camera when I had seen nothing with my own eyes. I had seen Tank, after all. Was the spirit orb separate from Tank — something unrelated to him? It seemed likely, because Tank hadn't been sitting by the painting, he'd been over next to the window. I hadn't thought to take a picture of the message written on the glass. Or I hadn't wanted to. Something about it wasn't sitting right with me.

"Mail call!" my computer chirped.

I was glad for the distraction. I clicked on the envelope icon, and was pleased to see Jac's name in my Inbox.

To: Voodoo Mama

From: Maestra

Well, we may be seeing each other sooner than planned. Can't go into it now, but there's been quite the blowup here. I'll call you when I'm home. Could be as soon as tomorrow morning.

And thanks for the picture of you and your tongue. What's with the light show? Peace,

Jac

Whoa. Jac coming home early? A blow-up? I could only imagine what that was supposed to mean.

Whatever had gone on, Jac would be back soon. I needed her here more than ever. Not being able to talk about the stuff going on next door was just about killing me.

My eye fell on the last line of Jac's e-mail. Light show? What was she talking about? The sentence seemed to be referring to the photo I'd e-mailed her. I minimized the e-mail screen and clicked through the photo images until I found the one I'd taken of myself.

There I was in all my glory, my dark hair

long and flat, my eyes slightly bugged, and my tongue stuck out at the camera. But that wasn't all the camera had captured. As I examined the picture, I could see right away what Jac's e-mail referred to.

Behind me, clearly visible, were circles of light. Not just one or two, but dozens of them. They were all over the place, but many of them were clustered just behind me. A shiver ran up my spine as I stared at the picture, transfixed.

My room was teeming with spirit orbs. Great.

I faked an upset stomach that night. I didn't feel good about these multiple episodes of being dishonest with my mother, but I had to have a reason to go to bed. She had a way of getting me to talk when I was upset about something. This time, I was determined to keep my fears to myself. I needed a convenient, noncontagious ailment that would explain my odd mood and my need to retreat from the world into the safe cocoon of my pillow and blanket. Stomach troubles covered all the bases, and required practically no further explanation.

My mom tucked me in, put a beeswax candle and a mug of peppermint tea by my bed, and lit a stick of Lord Buddha incense. Usually the familiar, heady scent instantly relaxed me, but at the moment I felt overwhelmingly anxious, as if something bad was going to happen.

"Is there anything else I can do for you, sweetie? Maybe a foot rub would help."

I shook my head and tried to smile.

"I just need to sleep, Mom," I said.

"Okay," she replied. "Try to drink some of the tea. It will help."

"I will," I told her.

She had to leave. If she didn't, if she stood looking down at me for one more minute with that concerned expression on her face, I was going to burst into tears. All those spirit orbs that had appeared in the photograph in my room — did she already know about them? Did they cluster around her, too? Why was I the only medium in the world who was scared of ghosts? I closed my eyes tightly, and tried to shoo the thoughts away.

"Sleep well, sweetie. Give a shout if you need anything."

I nodded, keeping my eyes closed. The telltale creak of the floorboards told me when she had walked out of my room. I lay absolutely still. I couldn't shake the feeling that I was being watched. That all those spirit orbs contained souls of people who were following me, trying to get my attention like a herd of celebrity-chasing paparazzi calling my name with the hope I would look their way.

"Leave me alone," I whispered.

I opened my eyes and stared at the candle by my bed. There was a golden halo of light around the flame — a hallmark of beeswax candles, so I'm told. On my chest of drawers, the tip of the incense glowed red. Downstairs I could hear quiet music. Everything was normal. Everything was safe.

So why was I still in such a state of panic?

There's a lake that I envision when I need to distract myself, or if I can't sleep. My happy place, if you want to call it that. It's a small lake surrounded by mountains and framed by pine trees. The water is astonishingly clear and warm. The sunlight there is more than warm and bright; it is alive somehow. It is intelligent and compassionate. The lake is a place of complete safety.

Even tonight, my lake worked its magic on me. My heart stopped pounding and the feeling of dread started to fade. One moment I was feeling the relaxing warmth of the imagined sun, and the next I had drifted off to sleep.

That's when the dreams started.

First I was in a concert hall. Jac was onstage, playing some kind of cello sonata. It was a difficult and emotional piece. Jac had long hair which flew about her head as she played. It almost looked like she was wrestling with the cello. I noticed someone standing in the wings and realized it was Jac's mother. Jac continued to play, but I noticed that her hands had begun to bleed. The cello seemed to be growing larger — so big that

Jac could barely support it. I was afraid the weight of it was going to crush her.

I wanted to call out to Jac to stop playing, but I was afraid. The concert hall was full of people, and Jac's mother was right up there, urging her on. Someone sitting behind me started laughing meanly. I turned around and recognized Brooklyn Bigelow. She was one of the "popular" girls from school — the one who had found out my mother was a medium earlier in the school year and used the information to try to humiliate me. Your classic mean girl. Brooklyn was pointing at Jac and snickering.

"She can't do it," Brooklyn was saying. "Look at her. She's going to pieces up there."

"Leave her alone," I hissed. "Just leave her alone!"

Brooklyn ran a hand through her highlighted hair and laughed. I was afraid to look back on the stage. I was afraid that Brooklyn was right, that Jac was literally coming apart onstage. I couldn't stand to see it happen. I got up and ran up the aisle and out of the auditorium. The dream changed.

I was at my lake. I could smell the pine trees and feel the gentle lake breeze on my face. A hummingbird flew past me, hovered nearby for a moment, then whizzed away. The lake itself was luminescent and peaceful. I walked closer to the water's edge and saw a boat in the water, tethered to a tree on the shore by a single white cord. There was someone in the boat. A small figure with soot-colored hair.

It was Tank.

I waded into the water, trying to get closer to him. The lake seemed to be expanding behind him. It was transforming itself into something huge, like an ocean. As the lake grew, the white cord stretched taut. The little boat rose and sank on waves that were growing increasingly larger.

I waded deeper. Somehow in the dream I knew I had to get to Tank before the cord broke and he was swept away from the shore. I had to get to him soon, or it would be too late. I struggled through the water. The sand fell away from beneath my feet. I was in over my head.

I heard something snap. The cord had broken, and the waves were carrying the boat away.

"Tank!" I called.

But I couldn't get to him. The boat grew smaller and smaller. I was treading water, and the waves were beginning to wash over my head. I had to swim back. I turned toward the shore. It was gone. There was nothing but water in every direction.

I woke up kicking and breathless, but I was safe in my own bed. The room had grown dark while I was asleep.

The candle, for some reason, had gone out.

Chapter 5

Jac called the next morning.

"You're back!" I exclaimed. "You have no idea how happy that makes me. I'm going off my nut around this house. You need to rescue me."

There was a pause.

"So what's going on?" I asked.

"I need to get out of here," Jac said. "I need to go somewhere where there are no musicians and no parents, and there are plenty of sweet, caffeinated drinks, and brownies the size of phone books."

"Can you get out of the house now?"

"Not even an act of God could stop me," Jac said. I noticed she was speaking very quietly, like she didn't want anyone to hear her. I imagined that Jac's mother trying to block the front door might be considered an act of God.

"I could meet you downtown. At the Bean Factory?" I asked, referring to our local version of Starbucks. I wanted to get away from my house, too.

"I can be there by ten thirty," Jac said. Now she was really whispering. "And promise me something, Voodoo Mama. For the first sixty minutes at the very least, swear you will not ask me about the conference, or mention the cello, or any stringed instrument."

"I swear," I said.

"Gotta hop," Jac whispered.

The line went dead.

Whatever was going on with Jac, it sounded serious. But I couldn't help feeling a sense of overwhelming relief. This was exactly the distraction I needed — and a reason to get out of the house and away from messages on windowpanes and clusters of spirit orbs.

I dressed quickly, dragged a brush through my dark tangles, and stared at myself in the mirror. There were circles under my eyes, not surprising since I'd had trouble getting back to sleep after my dreamfest. I put on a pair of my biggest, most dangly silver earrings to divert attention from the puffy circles. Makeup just wasn't an option. My mother never wore it, and the few times I'd tried it on, I'd felt like a clown.

The kitchen was empty, though my mother had left some freshly baked muffins out for me. I stuck my head around the door and could see that her office door was closed, meaning she had a client in for a spirit reading. Occasionally, my mother's sessions caused strange things to happen in the rest of the house — a sort of paranormal ripple effect. This was one morning that I categorically did not one to see one speck of supernatural activity, so I scrawled a note telling my mom where I was going and grabbed a muffin for the bus ride. I stopped in the living room to kiss Max, promised I'd take him for a long walk later, and presented him with a chunk of muffin.

I closed the front door quietly, the unfamiliar car in the driveway reminding me that my mother had someone in a session. I was on the sidewalk heading in the direction of the bus stop when I noticed that the man with the shaggy black and gray hair was back. He was standing in the same place I'd seen him the day before. A bike was leaning against the fence behind him.

I felt self-conscious, though he couldn't possibly know I'd spied on him through my camera's zoom lens. I walked down the sidewalk, trying to appear extremely interested in my muffin. But I sensed that the man was watching me from across the street. My curiosity got the better of me and I glanced over in his direction. He was looking at me. He raised his hand and waved, and I gave a little wave in response, but I quickened my pace. In a minute or so I'd reached the end of the block, and I turned right, the bus stop now in sight.

The bus was just pulling in. I sent silent thanks to the Universe for the convenience, as my mother had always taught me to do, and grabbed a seat near the back by a window. As the bus pulled out, I felt another wave of relief. For now, at least, I was leaving all my troubles behind.

When I got off the bus a block from the Bean Factory, I could see that Jac had already snagged a prime table outside. A hefty brownie, a chocolate milk, and a selection of little cookies were arranged on a plate in front of her. She was deeply engrossed in a magazine when I walked up to her.

"Maestra!" I called.

Jac looked up and squealed.

"Guess who's going to *jail*?"

My mouth dropped open. Things were apparently worse than I'd realized.

"Not . . . Jac . . . you don't mean . . . you?"

Jac looked momentarily enraged, then cracked up and swatted me with her *Star* magazine.

"Kat, please. Even my utterly disastrous life does not involve incarceration. No, it's Houston! Houston Ramada?"

Though I don't watch *Entertainment Tonight* or E! Television like Jac does, for once I actually knew who she was talking about. Houston Ramada was the poster child for celebrities famous for doing nothing but existing, serving no purpose but to annoy the rest of us. She was the main attraction in most of the glossy gossip mags, and Jac was addicted to celebrity gossip. It was an aspect of her personality that fit neither her position as a cello genius nor her preppy, conservative appearance. Hence, I loved it about her.

"I got you a frozen Mocha-Cho and a brownie. Sit down and listen to what this moron DID!"

Ah, yes. We had agreed to pretend that

nothing was going on with Jac, and I had decided to pretend that nothing was going on with me, for the next hour. I was more than happy to oblige.

"So she got her driver's license suspended, right? Remember, back in December?"

Jac was staring at me with the wide-eyed expression she reserved for the recounting of celebrity mishaps. Her red hair had been recently cut, exposing her tiny ears, and making her look even more pixielike than she usually did.

"And she got pulled over for speeding in January, and she claimed that she didn't realize that having your license suspended meant you couldn't drive!"

Jac paused to take a bite of a gigantic brownie, and I took a long, brain-freezing sip of my frozen Mocha-Cho.

"So then she gets pulled over again —
again — in February, and this time she says
her publicist told her that she *was* allowed
to drive again. So they make her sign this
paper, right? This paper that says that she
understands and accepts that she is *not*
allowed to drive until her license is rein-
stated. Right?"

I nodded emphatically, enjoying Jac's
increasingly frenzied delivery of the story.

"So last week, Houston goes to this Celebrity Car Wash event *driving* her Hum-
mer! And is totally surprised when she gets
busted!"

Jac paused here, waiting for me to say
something.

"Un-be-flipping-*lievable*!" I exclaimed.
This seemed to satisfy Jac, because she immediately continued.

"So now she's having this petition circulated, addressed to — and I'm not making this up — the Governor of California, saying that she was unfairly persecuted because of her celebrity status, and that sending her to jail is like this scandalous abuse of the justice system."

I nodded and made an outraged face, secretly delighted at Jac's moral fury.

"So apparently she really is going to jail for a couple weeks. She'll have to eat bologna sandwiches and wear an orange jumpsuit."

I snickered and took another long sip of Mocha-Cho.

"Schadenfreude," I said.

"What?"

"It was on our first vocabulary list this year. The month before you came to school. Schadenfreude. It means experiencing pleasure from something bad happening to someone else. It's a good word."

"It's fabulous," Jac proclaimed. Then she looked at her watch.

"Got a date?" I asked.

"Not in so many words," Jac said. "My mother thinks I'm at Miss Wittencourt's."

Miss Wittencourt was Jac's cello teacher — the one who had nursed her through her block earlier in the year when she suddenly couldn't play at all. She had also played an unwitting part in freeing the spirit of Suzanne Bennis, the young flute player who had haunted the library of our school. I still thought about that bizarre duet she had played with Jac — two performers, one living, one not. I felt the now familiar butterflies start up in my stomach.

No supernatural thoughts, I commanded myself. *Picture Houston Ramada behind bars. Picture Jac's mother behind bars.*

"Why does your mother think you're with Miss Wittencourt?" I asked.

"I have no idea," Jac said. "It might have something to do with the fact that that's what she told me to do."

"Oh," I said. It hadn't been sixty minutes yet, and this was technically becoming a cello-related conversation. But my curiosity got the better of me.

"Why did she tell you that?" I asked.

"She basically commanded me to go and see her today," Jac said, breaking off a bite-sized piece of brownie, then putting it back onto her plate. "Because of what happened at the conference."

"And . . . what did happen?"

Jac sighed, looking up and down the street.

"In a nutshell, it was a networking gig

for parents who are determined to lock their children into a lifetime of musical incarceration. There were seminars on how to increase your chances of getting into Julliard. Seminars on what the major orchestras are looking for in performers. Seminars on getting agents, on creating a distinctive performance personality, on the benefits of investing in a demo recording. Basically, it was a hundred different ways to completely sacrifice your daily existence to make it two percent more likely you'll become one of the tiny sliver of musicians who are able to earn a living in the field."

She paused, picked up the piece of brownie, then dropped it again.

"And here's the thing, Kat. Once again, no one ever asked me how I felt about this. No one ever said, 'Okay, Jac, this is what's involved. Is it worth it to you? Are you willing to live like this?' Nobody ever asks me what I want, Kat. Certainly my mother doesn't. She just makes her plans for me, like I'm . . . real estate, or something. I told you, remember, after the thing with Miss Wittencourt, that I had to decide if I wanted that scholarship. I had to decide if I wanted to play the cello at all."

I nodded. "I remember," I said.

"My mother talked for weeks about how there was so much I could get out of this conference, how . . . *valuable* it was going to be for me in the long run. That it could, like, change the entire course of my future. And I have to say, it's the first time she's been right about something in a long time."

"Because?"

"Because I did get something important

out of the conference. I finally knew what I needed to do. And I did it."

I waited. Jac crammed the brownie bite into her mouth and chewed it, like it was something she needed to destroy. She opened her carton of chocolate milk and took a swig. Then she carefully wiped the brown moustache off her upper lip and looked at me.

"I told my mother yesterday afternoon. And I promised her there was nothing in the world she could do to change my mind."

She reached across the table and grabbed my Mocha-Cho, taking a long sip through the straw. Something told me not to say anything or ask any questions. Jac was building up to something, and if I interrupted her she might never tell me. It was worth the painful sacrifice of the rest of my drink.

"And I feel so much better, Kat. Because I've finally done it."

She plunked the Mocha-Cho back in front of me and took a deep breath. Her eyes filled with tears.

"I've quit the cello."

My mouth dropped open. I couldn't believe what I was hearing. I'm not sure what surprised me more, that Jac had quit, or that she had openly defied her mother. Jac had talked about quitting before, but I never thought she'd actually do it. I thought it was just an option she needed to talk about, so that she felt more in control of her life. Jac and her cello were so deeply connected. She really was a genius. And she'd been playing almost all her life.

"I don't . . . I mean . . . are you okay?" I asked.

Jac nodded.

"I am more than okay, Kat. I'm better than I've been in years. I feel like this enormous burden has been lifted off my shoulders. I feel fabulous. I feel . . . free."

Then she burst into tears.

Chapter 6

I didn't know what to do. I had never seen Jac cry before. And she was doing it kind of loudly. People at other tables looked in our direction, curious.

I tried to think of something comforting to say, but I drew a blank. Instead, I held out my Mocha-Cho. Jac sniffled, rubbed at her eyes, then took the cup.

"Go ahead. Finish it," I said.

She did, sucking on the straw so hard her eyes bugged out a little. She finished the last quarter inch of the drink with a slurp and placed the empty cup on the table. Then she wiped the tears off her face.

"Oh, that's better," she said. "I hate getting all emotional like that."

"Well this is a huge deal," I said. "The cello is . . . the cello *was* a huge part of your life. It's like . . . well it's almost like you're getting divorced or something."

"No, I know. But this has been a long time coming, Kat. It's what I want. I'm not going to turn into a basket case over it. My mother, however, is another story."

"She must have gone ballistic," I said.

"Whatever," Jac said ruefully. "She can freak out 'til the cows come home. It won't change anything. I'm not going to play anymore, and nobody can make me."

"Does Miss Wittencourt know?"

"Please," Jac answered. "My mother called her from the conference. She tried to make me get on the phone with her, but I wouldn't. It's so pathetic, the way my mother thinks she has this power, or something. Like she can just blink, and I'll be exactly the person she wants me to be, with the ambitions she used to have, in the clothes she wants to wear."

Jac's phone rang, sounding the first few bars of Beethoven's Fifth.

"I've got to change this ringtone," she said, pulling out her phone and looking at the screen.

"Oh crud. It's her."

She flipped the phone open and answered it. I wasn't sure if "her" referred to Miss Wittencourt or Jac's mom, but as soon as Jac started talking there was no doubt who was on the other end of the phone.

"No, actually, I'm in town at a café. No, I didn't . . . No, I did not, Mother. You told me to go see Miss Wittencourt, and I left the house. I never actually said that I would . . . I don't care. I don't *care*! I'm out doing some things, and I'll come home when I'm done. . . . I don't *know*! Whenever I'm done is when I'll be done! I . . . you don't . . . I'm going, Mother. Goodbye."

Jac snapped the phone shut, pressing her lips tightly together.

"I'm guessing she's not very happy," I said.

"I can't stand this!" Jac exclaimed. "Like she thinks badgering me is going to change my mind? Like her nagging me every second of every day is going to make me say, 'Gosh, Mother, you were right. I made a huuuuuge mistake quitting the cello.' Why can't she just get her own life?"

I nodded sympathetically. From the few times I'd met Jac's mom, I'd found her to be cold, controlling, and more than a tad judg-mental, and she seemed to have no greater goal in life than pulling strings to advance Jac's musical career. No pun intended.

"She'll probably come looking for me now, or something. Can we go to your house, Kat? Please?"

I hesitated for just a moment. Even in the midst of all this drama, I was enjoying being away from my house, the spirit orbs, and Tank. But Jac looked so miserable, her ivory skin streaked with tears. She needed help, and she needed to get away from the Bean Factory. I wouldn't be at all surprised to see her mother striding down Main Street searching for her daughter.

"Of course we can," I said. "My mom was in a session when I left, but she'll probably be done by the time we get there."

"I don't even care," Jac said. "First of

all, you have a dog, who you promised was part *my* dog. Second of all, it could rain frogs and ooze ectoplasm all over your house — anything would be better than having to deal with *her*."

I wasn't so high on the frogs and ecto-plasm.

But that's just me.

The car that had been in our driveway when I left was gone, but my mother's office door was still closed. I was going to suggest to Jac that we bounce on the trampoline — it was an excellent way to rid oneself of anger. But the sky had been growing increasingly dark, and I heard a rumble of thunder in the distance.

"We should probably go upstairs until her session is over," I said, keeping my voice low and gesturing toward my mother's closed office door. Jac had made a beeline for Max and was kneeling next to him, her arms wrapped around his neck and her face pressed into his fur. She remained that way for a moment, then turned her face toward me. Just a minute of dog time had taken away some of the anxiety from her face.

"Anything you say, Voodoo Mama," Jac said. "Has your mom baked any of her wonderful cookies?"

It amazed me that Jac could still be hungry after the chocolate-fest at the Bean Factory. It also amazed me that for all her passionate love of desserts, she probably weighed about ninety pounds soaking wet.

"No cookies, but there are muffins," I said, leading Jac into the kitchen.

She made an exclamation of pleasure at the sight of the muffin plate and grabbed a large blueberry one. I took two glasses from the cupboard and a carton of milk from the fridge, and we went upstairs. Max, who hated thunderstorms, padded up the stairs behind us.

By the time we settled into my room, the rain was coming down in sheets against the window. It was the first good thunderstorm of the year. A flash of lightning was followed by thunder, and Max crept over to me, tail between his legs, hopped onto the bed between me and Jac, and curled himself into a tight ball.

"Jac, I'm so sorry about . . . everything that's going on. Tell me what I can do to help you."

Jac was stroking Max's back gently.

"It helps being here now, away from her," she replied. "It's only Wednesday — five more days of vacation. That's going to be the real challenge, Voodoo Mama. Figuring out how I'm going to survive at home for the rest of the week without going bonkers. My father is on a business trip in California until the day after tomorrow. Not that he's ever much help — he usually takes her side or doesn't take a side at all. This is like the only safe place there is right now."

"Well you can come over as often as you want," I said. "Come over every day."

"It's going to be tough," Jac said, shaking her head ruefully. "I'm telling you, Kat. She is on the *warpath.* I skipped out this morning, but it's not going to be that easy every day."

There was another clap of thunder outside. Max gazed up at me unhappily.

"It's okay, Max," I said, scratching his head between his ears. "It's only a storm. It's not going to hurt anything."

Max didn't look convinced.

"Hey, Jac, what about the basic communications project? What if we paired up and worked on it together?"

"Are we allowed to do that?"

"Definitely," I said. "As long as we both do the minimum amount of pages."

"Have you started?" Jac asked.

I nodded.

"So what's it about? What have you . . . what have *we* done so far, partner?"

She grinned at me, and I was relieved to see her looking marginally happy again.

Then I remembered Tank. And the spirit orbs.

I sighed.

"It's kind of complicated."

"Complicated in a way I'm going to like?" Jac asked.

I thought about Jac's strange serenity

when it came to encounters in the spirit realm.

"Actually, Jac, it's complicated in a way that probably only you alone would like. But it's a long story."

Jac leaned back regally on my pillows and got comfortable.

"Maestra is all ears, Voodoo Mama."

Chapter 7

I started with how I'd inadvertently caught Tank's face in a photo of the old house next door. Then I recounted my little trespassing venture, describing my experiences inside room by room. When I got to the part about the old man, Jac's eyes grew wide.

"Maybe he was possessed, you know, like in *The Exorcist*," Jac said. "Or maybe he murdered someone, and he doesn't want you to find out. Or maybe someone murdered him!"

This was another funny aspect about Jac's character. There was a whole realm of things that terrified her, mostly in the insect world. But with stories like this, Jac actually seemed to relish being scared. The creepier, the better.

"I got out of that room pretty fast, so I don't know," I said.

"Well, we'll have to go back," Jac said. I arched an eyebrow at her. Really? Go back? *We?*

"So you never found the boy in the picture?"

"No, I did find him. Sort of," I added. I explained how the boy had seemed completely unaware of me, despite my best efforts to get his attention. Then I described finding the message in the window — *help me.*

Jac clapped her hands together.

"Awesome! It's like that movie where the guy gets accidentally turned into a fly!"

I don't know where Jac found the time to

watch these ancient horror films, but she certainly had a commanding knowledge of them.

"And you came back here after that? Nothing else happened?" Jac asked.

I glanced over at my computer, thinking of the photograph of those spirit orbs clustered around me that had caused me to take to my bed with panic.

"Kat?"

I looked at my friend.

"What? Did something else happen?"

Max made a little whimpering noise in his throat. My mom and I call it sleep barking. He makes woof sounds, but without opening his mouth. And his feet twitch like he's running.

"Kat?"

"The picture I e-mailed you. You asked about the light show."

Jac nodded.

"Those are spirit orbs, Jac. Like, dozens of them."

"But you took that picture —"

"Here. In this room. And I have to tell you, I'm pretty freaked out about it."

"So your room is, like, outrageously haunted."

"I don't get the sense those orbs came with the room, Jac. I've never sensed anything in my room. I think they're attached to me. I think when I got the sight on my birthday, all of a sudden I kind of sent a signal to the underworld that I'm open for business. And they've flocked to me. It's me that's outrageously haunted. I'm pretty sure that these spirit orbs follow me wherever I go."

"Wait, so a spirit orb is like a ghost?"

"It's a soul. Sometimes a collection of souls."

"Which is different than a ghost?" Jac frowned in concentration.

"Yes. I mean, I'm not actually sure. It's — a ghost can be a number of things, right? Sometimes it's just energy. Like a shadow of a life that stayed after the life was gone. It's not an actual personality, just an echo. Then there are earthbound spirits. When they died, they might not have realized it. Or maybe they had such an intense belief that death was the end that they're unable to experience anything else. Um, trauma, like some really awful thing happening — that can cause a spirit to stay here rather than move on to the next level. And every once in a while there's just a bad egg."

"Like food poisoning?" Jac asked. Jac was terrified of getting food poisoning, and was the most rigorous inspector of expiration dates I'd ever known.

"No, I mean of the spirit variety," I said. "Think of some really bad person, who's totally obsessed with material things or physical things, you know, like drinking or something."

"Like Houston Ramada!"

"Well, yeah in a way, but I'm thinking of someone more, you know, evil than ditzy. Someone even worse than Brooklyn Bigelow. Someone who derives all her power from having money or controlling people. You see, when someone like that dies, she may refuse to move on. Physical life is where she has all her power, and she doesn't want to know any other kind of existence. So she hangs around, either manifesting as a ghost, or looks for someone vulnerable to act as a host."

"A host?"

"Yeah ... like, a person to sort of live

through. Someone she can invade, and kind of occupy her consciousness a little bit. It's sort of like that cartoon where the guy has an angel on one shoulder, and a devil on the other. The spirit would act as the bad influence on one shoulder, trying to encourage the host to do what the spirit wants. Like control other people, or get lots of money or eats tons of food or something."

Jac drew her knees up to her chin.

"Kat, I was just *kidding* about the possession thing. Now you're telling me it's actually possible?"

I sighed.

"I don't know, Jac. I really don't. The spirit world isn't that simple. My mom thinks it's possible for a negatively charged energy or spirit to become attached to a human to try to influence that person. But not everyone believes that can happen. My mom says some psychics and mediums don't think it's possible."

"Do you believe it?"

Jac was almost whispering.

"I don't think I can afford not to," I said. "I feel like I have to be on my guard."

"Why?"

I got up and went over to my computer. With a few clicks of the mouse, I pulled up my most recent photos. I found the one of me sticking my tongue out, and maximized it to fill the entire screen.

"Because of this," I said.

Jac slid off my bed and joined me next to the computer.

"The spirit orbs," she said.

I nodded.

"They all want something from me. And

for all I know, there are more arriving every moment," I said.

"You don't see them right now?" she asked.

I shook my head.

"No. But they're there. I'm not just saying that because of the picture. Seeing the photograph was kind of a wake-up call. It tuned me in to it. They're not manifesting or trying to communicate right now. But I feel them, Jac. I feel them everywhere. They're all over me. They're all around me. And they want me to let them in.

"I'm going nuts — I want to jump right out of my skin. It's like . . . having cooties or something. Except that I'm, like, terrified of them. I think it's partly because of that old man. All that rage coming off of him. I don't want to have anything to do with a spirit like that. But apparently what I want doesn't matter. They're here. And I have no idea what to do about it."

My voice started to shake a little bit. My heart was racing slightly, and the nausea returned. Just talking about it made me want to unzip my body like a suit and run far, far away. Jac put her hand on my arm.

"Well, you know about one of them, right? Tank appeared to you. Tank seems to have reached out for help. So let's start with him. Tank is one spirit that you can do something about."

"Can I, though?" I asked. "I went over to the house, Jac, and I figured I'd find the answer there. Or that at least I'd find out what I was supposed to do next. But I came up totally empty. Tank won't communicate directly with me. How can I possibly help him?"

Jac looked thoughtful.

"I guess you're going to have to find out

who he is," she said. "Then maybe you can find out how he died. That's what we did with Suzanne Bennis. And once we knew that Miss Wittencourt's guilt and sadness was keeping her here, you knew how to help her move on. So first we have to know Tank's story."

I sighed.

"Any suggestions?"

"You said the date on Tank's painting, the one his aunt Ruby did, was dated a few years back."

I nodded.

"So you have a date, at least, when you know he was living in the house. You've been in this house two years. Tank's family was probably the last family to live there before the house went empty."

"Possibly. But we don't know who they were, Jac. We don't even know their names."

"There must be a way to find out. Like, town records or something."

"I don't know anything about town records. What would we do, call the town hall and ask about aunt Ruby?"

Jac shrugged, a small smile on her face.

"Don't you know anybody else on this street that might remember them?

I shook my head.

"We're not exactly the outgoing, host-a-neighborhood-barbecue kind of family," I said. "I don't know any of my neighbors."

Jac suddenly sat up very straight, her eyes wide.

"I know! How about we go outside and see if there's a name still on the mailbox?"

I stared at Jac, my mouth slightly open.

She smiled, making her appear even more elfin than usual.

"You may express your gratitude for my brilliance by supplying more baked goods," Jac declared grandly.

"Then we'd better go to the kitchen."

Jac was already at the door.

Chapter 8

"I don't see why we can't wait until the rain stops," I complained.

I pulled a rain poncho over my head, generating a field of static electricity that caused the hair on the crown of my head to stand straight up.

Jac pointed at me and laughed.

"Kat! You look adorable with a mohawk!"

"This is the thanks I get for letting you wear my raincoat?"

Jac grinned and pulled a ball cap over her

red hair. The hat was big on her — she looked like she was about eight years old.

"Ready?" she asked.

I glanced back in the direction of my mother's office.

"It's fine, Kat," Jac said. "We'll only be gone two minutes. She won't get worried."

"I know," I said. "It's just that I don't understand why her door is still closed. There's no other car parked out there."

"Maybe she's meditating," Jac suggested.

"She does that at dawn," I replied.

"Come on!" Jac said, pulling me by the arm.

I submitted to Jac's pressure. It was like being pulled by a tiny bird or a miniature poodle. But the force of her personality far exceeded the force of her little arms.

I opened the front door and we walked outside. The rain had let up a little, but it was still coming down fairly steadily. Jac led the way, and I followed her obediently onto the sidewalk, feeling like a puppy.

The house had a fairly regulation mailbox — a black metal structure shaped like a loaf of bread, with a door on the front and a red flag that you raised if you wanted the postman to pick up mail. I couldn't see any lettering on the side that faced our house. Jac walked around the other side.

"Here!" she said.

I moved to where Jac stood, and bent down to examine the mailbox. There were no letters there now, but an outline of the letters that had once been there, and presumably peeled off, were legible.

"V-A-N," I read, squinting.

"H . . . is that an E?" Jac asked.

"Yeah, E-C-M . . ."

"I think that's an H." Jac rubbed several fingers over the surface of the mailbox to wipe the water away.

"Okay, H, and the last letter is T."

"Van Hecht," said Jac. "There was a conductor named van Hecht, I think."

"It's a pretty distinctive name," I said. "Can't imagine there are too many van Hecht families in this neck of the woods. So it might actually be easy to trace. Let's go back to my house. I'm getting soaked. My socks are wet."

"Hang on," Jac said. She was peering at the front door of the house.

"Jac . . ."

"I just want to go up and touch the door."

"Jac, that's stupid. It's probably locked."

"I just want to touch it," Jac said. "It's my first haunted house!"

I was getting wetter by the second, and I was beginning to feel chilly, too. But there was no dissuading Jac from an idea once she had it. The fastest thing would be to just let her do her thing so we could get inside.

"Okay, then. Come on."

Jac clapped her hands together like a kid trying to prove she still believes in fairies.

I shook my head, but inwardly I was amused. Jac was turning into a regular junior ghost hunter. I liked the idea of having her as my sidekick.

We reached the door, and I put my hand on it.

"Well, there it is. A regular door. Have a touch, and let's go!"

Jac placed her hand on the door, palm flat and fingers spread, just below a brass door knocker.

"Spirit vibes," she said, eyes wide.

"Wouldn't surprise me one bit," I said. "Can we go now?"

Jac pulled her hand off the door, but then she grabbed the door knocker and rapped it loudly.

Bam. Bam. Bam.

"What are you doing?" I asked. "There's no one in there, Jac."

She turned to me, her face shining.

"Maybe the house will let us in," she said.

I sighed. I waited. Nothing happened.

"It doesn't work that way. Nobody's home," I said. "Come on. Are you ready?"

Jac looked wistfully at the door, then turned to me.

"Okay. Yeah. Let's go."

We were three or four steps down the walkway when we both stopped in our tracks.

The red flag on the mailbox had been raised.

The flag that moved by itself was apparently enough of a brush with the supernatural for Jac for the time being. She beat a hasty retreat, speeding back up the walkway to my house and yanking open the front door. By the time I'd gotten my coat off, Jac was already halfway up the stairs to the second floor.

When I got to my room, Jac was taking a seat by the computer.

"I thought you wanted to encounter spirit vibes," I said reproachfully.

Jac turned to look at me. Her face was shining.

"Are you kidding? I totally did. That was

awesome! Tank might not be able to speak to you, Kit Kat, but something is certainly trying to get your attention."

"Then why did you zip back to my room at the speed of light? I thought you must have gotten freaked out."

Jac shook her head firmly.

"I'm looking for the family," she said, her fingers tapping on the keys.

"You're just going to Google van Hecht?"

"Lexis Nexis," Jac replied. "Practically every newspaper and magazine in the country is linked through this. If a child died in that house, it probably made the local newspapers, right? I'm telling it to search this town, the name van Hecht, and giving it a time parameter of the last five years."

Jac seemed to know exactly what she was doing, and I was happy to let her take the lead. I walked to the window and looked outside. The rain had stopped abruptly and the sun shone through a break in the clouds, illuminating the drenched landscape in celestial light. Tank's house stood silently. From the safety of my bedroom, I could detect no movement or energy inside. The house itself seemed solid and almost friendly, the way really old houses sometimes do.

"Okay, got something," Jac said excitedly.

I reached her chair in two huge steps.

"Where? What?"

Jac pointed to an article.

"I found a couple listings for your van Hechts that were dated three years ago. There was some kind of traffic accident."

"Tank was in a traffic accident?" I asked.

Jac scrolled down the page.

"His brother was. Listen: 'On Wednesday

evening Julius van Hecht, son of Greta and Theodore van Hecht of Seth Avenue, was struck by a car while riding his bicycle. Witnesses recount that the car, which fled from the scene, had driven through a stop sign. Julius suffered severe head injuries and was airlifted to Philips Memorial Hospital, where he remains in critical condition.'"

I tried to ignore the disturbing visual image of a little boy being struck by a speeding car from my mind.

"Well, this house is on Seth Avenue, and there's only one stop sign. It's just one block up, where you turn to get to the bus stop. That must be where it happened. What else does it say?"

"Nothing much, but let me check the next article. It was written a few days later. It's shorter. It just says that Julius remains in a coma at Philips Memorial, and that the police are looking for the driver of the car that hit him."

So the van Hechts had experienced two tragedies. Julius had been hit by a car and fallen into a coma. And at some point, Tank had died.

"Okay, here's the last article I found. It was written on the one-year anniversary of the accident. It says that Julius is still in a coma, and that the doctors are uncertain whether he will ever recover. And it also says that the van Hechts moved from their house on Seth Avenue and took an apartment over in Robertstown to be closer to the hospital. And that the mom still sits with Julius every day, and talks to him. They never caught the guy who did it."

"No wonder they left," I said, staring in the direction of the van Hecht house. "Can you imagine losing two children?"

"They didn't lose Julius," Jac said. "I mean, he's still alive."

"You think he still is? Lying in a coma in that hospital?"

"No other articles came up," Jac said.

"Maybe Tank died after they moved away," I mused. "If he died in Robertstown that would explain why it didn't show up in our local paper."

"And he's come home. To the house he grew up in," Jac said.

I nodded.

"Geez. This is depressing me."

"Think how I must feel, Jac. I'm surrounded by dead people."

Jac looked at me sympathetically. Then she looked at the space above my head, like she was trying to get a glimpse of a spirit orb.

"I could take another picture of you," Jac

said. "We could see how many orbs show up now."

"I'd really rather not," I said.

"Well, let's walk down the block, then," Jac suggested. "The sun's finally out. Maybe if we go to that stop sign, you'll pick up something more about the van Hechts. You know, maybe Tank was even there when it happened. Maybe the accident is what's keeping him in the house. He could feel responsible, or something."

Jac was getting better and better at this ghost hunting game. It was a good suggestion. The thought of looking for the place where Julius's accident had occurred gave me the creeps, but I had to move on with Tank's story or I wouldn't be able to help him. The only lead we had on Tank was what happened to Julius. Once again, Jac seemed to know the best thing to do.

"Okay," I said. "Let's take Max. He's already traumatized from the storm."

Max had gotten off my bed and was standing by my bedroom door. I had grown accustomed to Max knowing when I was going to suggest a walk before the thought actually entered my mind.

We went downstairs and I grabbed his leash from the hook in the hallway. My mother's door was still closed, though I could hear voices now. What was going on in there? Nobody ever showed up for a session without a car. Maybe they'd taken a taxi?

Max pulled me gently toward the door. Jac brushed past me, bent to kiss Max on the nose, and opened the door, bounding lightly down the steps to the walkway. Max and I followed, almost colliding with Jac, who had come to a dead stop where the sidewalk began.

"Cripes, Maestra, make up your mind — are you running or standing still?"

Jac said nothing. I felt her stiffen, or more like I sensed her energy freezing. She was staring down the street in the direction of Julius's stop sign.

"Don't tell me you actually see something," I said cheerfully. "Just because you've quit the cello doesn't mean you can start seeing ghosts. That's my unique brand of insanity. Jac?"

She wasn't smiling. Looking down the street in the direction of her gaze, I immediately realized why.

A car was approaching. I could see the driver's face — Jac's mother. The car pulled up alongside our driveway. The door opened, and Jac's mother stepped out of the car. She was thin and red-haired like Jac, but much taller. She was dressed in her usual conservative fashion: khaki pants, a pale pink oxford shirt, and a sweater draped over her shoulders. Pearls. Espadrille shoes. Her face was white, frozen, and her expression was one of silent and dangerous anger.

"Get in the car, Jackie," she said in a low voice.

"Hi, Mrs. Gray — Jac's actually partnering with me on the basic communications project. We're doing a mixed media history of that —"

"Get in the car now," Jac's mother repeated. It was as if I hadn't spoken. It was as if I wasn't standing there at all.

There was this moment when everything was frozen. Nobody spoke. Even Max didn't seem to be breathing. Anything could have happened. I braced myself for an explosion.

But what happened next was the last thing I expected.

Without a word, Jac climbed into the back of the car.

Seconds later, Jac's mother started the ignition, and they sped off down the street. Jac's face, small and white, peered out the rear window at me. I stood there, speechless. It was absolutely quiet, like the world was trying to adjust to what had just happened. The silence was interrupted by the sound of my front door closing. I turned around to look.

Someone was coming out of my house.

Chapter 9

It was the shaggy-haired man that I'd stalked with my camera.

We stared at each other. His face was pleasant and open, lips turned up in a smile that accentuated the lines on his face. I don't know what my expression said. What I was thinking was — *What in the world was that guy doing in my mother's office? A guy? A . . . somewhat hot guy?*

My father left Mom and me abruptly three years ago. You hear a lot about a thing called a "mid-life crisis," and it sounds totally hokey. But I'm here to tell you it is real. There's just no other excuse for what he did to us. My father was really different than my mom. He didn't believe in God, let alone spirit guides and trans-dimensional communication. But I guess they cared about each other. Once. They had fun. Until they stopped having fun. And the mid-life crisis started.

First it was an earring. My father, who worked for an accounting firm and was pretty much a suit-and-tie guy, came home with a silver stud in his ear. Mom and I thought it was great. Then he started running every morning. Lifting weights. Went to a tanning salon. Bought a motorcycle. That was about the time he started working late. And even though he seemed to be totally indulging his every whim and desire (it was a very big motorcycle), he went to my mom one day and told her he wasn't happy.

That was it. One minute he wasn't happy, and the next week he was packing his bags. We were supposed to believe that the woman who came to pick him up the day he moved out, a perky blonde named (I kid you not) Chickie, was just a friend. Whatever. They live together now, in Florida. He doesn't send birthday cards or Christmas cards. Or money.

I have this ocean of rage toward my dad. I hate not having a father. I hate that we were so disposable to him. I hate that I look much more like him than I do my mother. But what burns me the most is the way he just cast my mother off. She's much cooler with it now than I am. Don't get me wrong, she's not happy about it. She doesn't speak fondly of him, or make excuses, or pretend like it was partly her fault. But after a year or so, she accepted what had happened.

She said she'd carried it around long enough, and she just cast all her hurt and resentment into the Universe, and moved on. And even though I was still mad as all get out, I was glad that she was able to get back to her present and her future. After all, we still had each other. And we were fine, just the two of us. I was happy with the way things were.

But I wasn't the least bit prepared to see a cute guy coming out of her office.

All this was going through my mind as I looked at the shaggy-haired guy. Which is why I have no idea what my expression looked like. And why I had no idea what to say.

"Hey," said cute shaggy guy.

I could have come up with that.

"Hey," I replied. I tried to look casual, but I could feel my brow furrowing in suspicion.

"You must be Kat," he said. He took a few steps toward me, then stopped about three feet away. Close enough for me to see that his eyes were a brilliant, sparkling blue.

I nodded. I felt absurdly lucky to be Kat at that moment.

"I'm Orin," he said.

I had no response for this magnificent piece of information. Max pulled on the leash a little until I gave him some slack. He walked right up to Orin, sniffed his knees, then curled up at Orin's feet. I felt a stab of peculiar jealousy. This was a strange guy who had been in my house. Why was Max cozying up to him? It's not like we knew for a fact he wasn't an axe murderer.

"Your mom and I did a few energy and healing seminars together a couple years ago," Orin continued. "I was in the neighborhood, and I just happened to see her out by the driveway this morning, walking someone to their car. Couldn't believe it was her. We've been sort of going over old times."

I nodded again. Mom sometimes went to seminars and conferences of a spiritual or metaphysical nature. I couldn't remember her mentioning Orin, but she might have. I could have forgotten the name. The face, I would not have forgotten.

"I do energy work," Orin continued, since I was doing nothing to hold up my end of the conversation. "Reiki, polarity work, healing, stuff like that."

"Right," I said, nodding. Like he'd gotten an answer correct or something.

In spite of myself, I kept glancing over at

the van Hecht house. When I had first seen Orin, he'd seemed to be watching that house. Or maybe he was just lost, or he saw a red-tailed hawk on the roof or something. But the thing is, he noticed me looking at the house. Because he started glancing over at it, too. I wanted to get away from Orin all of a sudden. I wanted to go back into that house.

"Anyway," I said, looking pointedly in the opposite direction from the van Hecht house, "I should probably get back inside."

Orin nodded. He gave me a smile that left me slightly weak in the knees.

"I expect I'll see you around," he said.

"Yeah," I replied. Part of me wanted to shout it — pump a fist in the air. YEAH!!

He started to turn, then he looked back at me.

"I teach, too, you know. I was actually

just talking to your mom about that. I don't take on too many students, but when I find someone who . . . well, if there's a person who seems to have an unusual ability, somebody particularly gifted . . ."

"Right," I said. Was he talking about me? Had he and my mom been talking about my spirit sight?

"Yeah. Anyway. Something to keep in mind."

"Right," I said again. I was an A student in English. I'd aced every spelling and vocabulary assignment of the year. Why couldn't I think of any other English words except for right?

"Right," Orin repeated. "Your fifth chakra is blocked, by the way. See ya 'round."

He walked past me and crossed the street. His bike was leaning up against the face where it had been yesterday. Max stood up and took a few steps after him. Traitor dog, I thought, tightening my grip on the leash.

And what the heck kind of thing was that to say to somebody? Your fifth chakra is blocked, by the way — see ya 'round.

I knew a little about the chakras, but they were more my mom's thing. They're like little spinning spiral disks of energy in our bodies. We have seven of them. Each one represents a different thing. And when one is blocked, the energy can't flow through your body right. It's like throwing a tree down into a stream — it gunks up the works. The fifth chakra was the throat chakra. It was connected with being true to yourself, connecting with your divine source, and stuff like being who you're supposed to be.

If my mother was friends with Orin, then he was definitely the real thing, not a quack. So my fifth chakra was blocked. I was withholding truth. I was turning my back on self-knowledge.

Big whoop.

I was starting to feel like an idiot, standing there on the sidewalk. Orin was kneeling down next to his bike, fiddling with something — a lock, maybe. I couldn't just keep standing there. But I didn't want to go back inside. Then I'd have to talk to my mother. She'd tell me more about Orin. For some reason, I didn't want to hear it. I don't know if I was embarrassed or envious, but I just didn't want to know what she and Orin had been talking about all that time in her office. Maybe it was because I was afraid they'd been talking about me. Maybe it was because I was afraid they hadn't.

I headed around the back of my house, unlatching the gate that led into our little garden and yard. I let Max off his leash and stood with my arms folded, trying to decide what to do next. Before I could even seriously mull the prospects over in my mind, my feet started moving of their own accord. In sixty seconds I was standing in the overgrown yard in back of the van Hecht house.

I needed a place to hide. I needed to be somewhere that no one would find me for a while. Away from the phone, away from my perfect mother. From shaggy-haired guys on bikes. From spirit orbs swarming around me and blocked chakras. Something kept telling me that Tank held the answer. Though I wasn't even sure what the question was.

I opened the screen door the same way I had the day before. The kitchen window was still propped open. I didn't think anyone had been to the house since my last visit. I climbed through and stood in the empty kitchen, wondering what on earth I was doing there.

I had just started to think that I was being ridiculous to avoid home and that I should just go talk to Mom when the kitchen window slammed shut with a bang so loud I screamed. On the porch, the screen door flew open and shut several times. The windchimes fell to the floor in a heap.

I backed away from the window, pressing one hand over my pounding heart. As I took several cautious steps backward, the cupboard doors flew open, one at a time, like a row of dominoes. When the last one opened, the first snapped closed with a crack, and the others followed suit.

I ran through the dining room and the hall, and stopped by the front door of the house. My heart was pounding even harder, and I was short of breath. I tried the front door, which was locked. Through the window I could see the mailbox. The flag was down again. Something made several loud popping sounds in the kitchen, then I heard the sound of a chair being dragged across the floor. The next noise I heard came out of my own throat. It was a tight whimper of one hundred percent fear.

The sitting room had given me an okay vibe, I remembered. A child had played in there. In four giant steps I was out of the hallway and in the old sitting room. No ball. The room was empty. And freezing.

Something grabbed hold of the back of my shirt and yanked sharply.

I screamed again, backing out of the room and swatting my hands in the air as if

I was being attacked by bees. I turned in the direction of the kitchen, wanting nothing more than to get out of the house as quickly as possible. But I was stopped by the sound of a crash from that direction, and what sounded like a heavy piece of furniture being dragged across the floor.

I ran up the staircase, freezing at the top of the landing. The old man's room was up here. But I didn't want to go back downstairs. I didn't want to go back to the kitchen. I was literally stunned with terror, my breath coming in short shallow gasps. If it really was possible to die of fright, then I'd have been dead at that moment.

Something had *touched* me in the living room. Grabbed me. I had never been physically touched by a spirit. My mother had never said such a thing was possible. If a thing down there could grab my shirt, what else could it do? Shove me down the stairs? Put its hands around my throat?

I was crying now, at least as much as I could cry between gasps for breath. My face felt prickly and strange, and I was dizzy and nauseated. I felt like I was going to throw up. I stumbled into the third bedroom, the only one I hadn't been inside yet, only to be hit by a wall of air so cold it took my breath away. I turned to get away from the room and came face-to-face with the old man, who had appeared in the doorway. His face was contorted with rage. He opened his mouth, but no words came out. Instead he uttered a kind of howl, the cry of an animal in pain and terror.

This was, as they say, the last straw. I opened my mouth and screamed longer and louder than I thought physically possible, determined to drown him out. I closed my eyes tightly, and backed further into the room, finally pressing myself into the corner. I wedged myself there with my hands up by my face, and kept screaming, over the sound of breaking glass in the distance. The floor was spinning, and something was coming up the stairs, heavy and fast. The last thing I remembered was opening my eyes and looking into the startled face of Orin.

Then I guess I passed out.

Chapter 10

I woke up on the old wicker couch on the van Hechts' porch. I was still feeling sick to my stomach.

"Stay still," I heard. "Don't try to sit up yet."

I didn't try to look up at Orin. I honestly felt like I was dying.

"There's something wrong with me," I said, barely whispering. "It's hard to breathe . . . I feel really weird . . ."

"You're having a panic attack, Kat," Orin said. "Will you let me help you?"

Anything was better than feeling like this. I nodded.

"Close your eyes," Orin said. "Take a deep breath through your nose, and slowly let it out through your mouth. While you're breathing in, think *soooooo*. While you're breathing out, think *hummmmmm*. Try not to think about anything else. Just the breathing, and those two words."

It sounded ridiculously stupid, but I was desperate. I did as he instructed. After a minute or so, miraculously, I began to feel a little better. And the fact that I did feel a little better made me realize that maybe I wasn't going to die. But a panic attack? I didn't even know what that was, but it sounded kind of pathetic.

"Sooo . . . hum . . ." Orin reminded me. "Your color's coming back, Kat. Keep focusing on the breath."

I didn't feel sick to my stomach anymore. The prickly feeling I'd had all over my skin was going away. I opened my eyes and peeked at Orin. His forehead was crinkled, his eyes concerned. He was holding both hands out, palms facing me.

"What are you doing?" I asked.

"Giving you some help," Orin explained, lowering his hands. "Energy work."

"But you didn't touch me."

"It's not necessary. Your energetic field extends beyond your physical body."

Okay. Who was somebody who saw dead people to find somebody who did energy work weird?

"How did you find me in there?"

"I heard you," Orin said. "Well, I heard something. I didn't know it was you. But I heard someone scream. I broke the front window and unlocked the door. Followed the sound, and found you in the bedroom."

"He was coming for me," I said. "The old man. I think he wanted to hurt me."

Orin waited to see if I was going to say anything else.

"I'm not crazy," I added defensively. "He was here. He . . ."

"I don't think you're crazy," Orin said.

"Before I went upstairs," I said. "I . . . the house started to go ballistic. Things slamming and crashing. Okay, I know it sounds nuts, Orin, but somebody grabbed me. I felt it. Seriously. I wanted to run out the back door, but there was something there. I couldn't go that way. It was like the house wanted to drive me upstairs."

Not the house, I thought suddenly. The old man. I couldn't prove it, but I was certain he'd been behind the series of events that had sent me running up the stairs. The old man wanted me for some reason. To tell me something, or show me something. I was more determined than ever not to let that happen.

Orin was watching me carefully, his head cocked to one side. Then he spoke.

"I know. I could feel the energy — it was riled up and swirling like a hurricane. Kat, you have a mediumistic gift."

"I know that," I said, stupidly feeling defensive.

"Let me finish. I know it's come to you recently."

I nodded.

"Coming into a gift like yours is a delicate business, Kat. The conditions of your life have changed. There are things you'll need to know. And there are things you'll have to experience in order to learn."

Great.

"I told you before that your fifth chakra was blocked. I'm getting the sense that you're fighting them, Kat."

"The spirits?"

Orin nodded.

"I'm not sure what you mean."

"Okay. Let me think of how to put this. . . . A few months ago, your energetic system totally changed. Imagine you're a radio. And the only signal you've ever received is . . . some easy listening station. Then one day, blam — you start receiving another station, and another, and another, and tons of information and sounds and sights are being broadcast to you — ones you aren't accustomed to.

"And at the same time, *you* start putting out a signal — you're like a beacon. Spirits can sense your portal is open. So they start flocking to you. Maybe the first couple of times you manage it. But now they're lining up — they're all trying to get your attention.

"You don't know how to handle it — you're not even sure you *want* to handle it. So you start throwing out these energetic blocks. You're not sending the spirits away; you're just making it harder for them to be heard. So they start trying harder to get your attention. And harder. The more determined you are to shut them out, the more determined they are to be heard. It explains what happened in the house — the things slamming. The physical sensations. I'm guessing that was one very determined spirit."

Was this guy a healer or a psychic? How

could he know all this about me because one stupid chakra was blocked?

"The old man," I said. "He's not the only spirit here, but he's off his head with anger. I don't think he can control it. I can't . . . I'm scared of him. I'm afraid he'll hurt me. He's definitely one I'm resisting."

Orin nodded. I was sort of hoping he'd give me a little lecture about how a spirit couldn't physically harm a human, but he didn't.

"Is the old man making me feel sick and dizzy like this?" I asked. After all, Orin seemed to have the answers to everything else. "This isn't the first time I've felt this way, either. It was way worse this time, but I've had all this for a couple of days — the pounding heart, and feeling sick, plus feeling like a giant Band-Aid is being yanked off my skin."

Orin had been kneeling next to the wicker couch. Now he shifted, sitting on the floor with his legs extended.

"Your physical body and your energetic body are connected," Orin said. "The resisting, and the blocks you're putting out, and probably the anxiety it's all causing you, basically make your body overheat, like a car engine. The fight or flight mechanism kicks in. Your heart beats faster, you produce a bunch of adrenaline, and that makes you feel shaky, which is scary, which makes your heart beat even faster, and so on. It's a vicious cycle. But the deep breathing can stop it."

I sighed. Breathing did feel good. I'd never really thought about it before.

"I guess you'll want to know what I was doing in the house in the first place," I said.

"Not if you don't want to tell me," Orin replied.

Ah.

"Well, I kind of guess I maybe don't at this moment," I said. "I'd kind of like to get some space between me and the . . . things in there. That man."

Orin nodded.

"Sounds like a wise choice."

I started to get to my feet, but Orin cautioned me with one raised hand.

"Just stay sitting a minute. Breathe."

I complied.

"A panic attack is traumatic to your body. You need to take it easy. Not just right now, but for the rest of the day. I wouldn't explore any more abandoned houses if I were you."

"Trust me, that won't be a problem, Orin," I said dryly. Then I stood up carefully. When the floor didn't rush up to smack me in the head, I knew I was probably okay. Orin opened the screen door for me and followed me down the back steps into the yard.

"Think about what I said, Kat."

"Which part?"

"My teaching. I can help you to learn to manage your energy. I can teach you how to throw a kind of frequency bubble up around yourself when you want some space from the spirits. So your system doesn't overload like it has been. It's not good for you to be constantly in a state of fear, Kat. Your spirit sight is a divine gift, not a curse. I can help take the fear out of it for you. Nobody should have to be so frightened of who they are."

"I'll think about it, okay?"

Orin nodded.

"I'm just going to climb the wall back into my yard," I said, nodding toward my house.

"I'm going to go back in the house to

clean up the glass," Orin said. "Take care of yourself."

I watched Orin go back onto the porch and disappear into the kitchen. Then I turned and walked toward the wall.

My mother was walking down the back steps toward the garden. She was looking right at me.

I froze, one foot perched partway up the stone wall. Had she seen me come out of the house with Orin? Did it matter if she did? I couldn't understand why I felt so secretive about Orin and everything that came close to the van Hecht house. I couldn't understand why I needed to keep so many things from my mother these days.

"More work for your school project?" she asked.

"Kind of," I replied, climbing over the wall and hopping down into our yard. It could be true. It wasn't at the moment, but maybe I could make it true.

"What happened to Jac?"

I was relieved to have the subject moving away from the van Hecht house. Probably she hadn't seen me with Orin, then.

"Her mother came and abducted her," I said. "She's gone totally nuclear because Jac told her she's quitting the cello."

"Oh boy. Poor Jac," my mother said. I nodded.

"Anyway, that's it. Jac's gone. I might try to e-mail her to find out what's happening, since I have a feeling her mother won't be letting her use the phone. In fact, I think I'll go send her one right now."

I started toward the house, again uncertain why I was in such a hurry to get away from my mother. Her kindness, her goodness, the way she was so different from

Jac's mom, all of that was making me mad. Go figure. I felt angry at my mom because she was such a nice person, and that made it painful to shut her out.

"Kat?"

I stopped and looked at her over my shoulder.

"Is there some reason you're leaving out part of the story?"

I looked at her and raised my eyebrows.

"Huh?"

"Five minutes ago you were standing in the yard next door with Orin. Were you going to mention that you'd met him?"

I opened my mouth to reply, but nothing came out. Because I didn't have an answer for her. I didn't even have an answer for myself.

She walked toward me and stood close, brushing my hair out of my eyes.

"Maybe I'm imagining things. But these last few weeks, especially these last few days, I feel like you're putting up walls. Shutting me out. I get the sense that there are things going on with you that you feel it's important you keep from me. And that worries me. You're entitled to your privacy, Kat, like anyone else. But I'm worried about you."

I couldn't tell her she was wrong. Because she wasn't wrong.

But I sure didn't want to tell her she was right.

Chapter 11

Typical me. Since I didn't know what to say, I cried instead. And I don't mean a tear or two trickling down my cheek. I bawled. I cried for Tank, and for Jac. I cried for my mom, raising me all by herself. I cried for me, too — for the part of me that was terrified of my spirit sight, and for the part of me that couldn't seem to confide in my mother anymore.

During all this sobbing, my mom put her arm around my shoulders and led me inside. She sat me down at the kitchen table and put a kettle on for some tea. When my bawling downgraded into sobs, and then sniffles, she wet a cool cloth and handed it to me. I pressed my face into it. The cold and wet sensation helped shock me back into myself. My mother placed a steaming cup of tea in front of me. Its familiar smell was comforting. I had a few more sniffles in me, and then I felt almost like myself again. Myself with a swollen face and red eyes.

"Who is Orin, anyway?" I asked.

She didn't seem to mind that having left so many of her questions unanswered, I now had one for her.

"He's a healer," she said. "I got to know him four or five years ago — you remember when I did that six-week intensive program at the Omega Institute? He was there, too. After that, I ran into him at a couple other programs. We were friends. But after your dad, after the move and everything, we lost touch. Things got complicated."

By complicated, my mom meant that cash was too tight for any more new age workshops, and anyway a single mother couldn't up and leave her daughter to take classes at the Omega Institute. I felt a flash of anger at my father. He had taken away so much from both of us.

"I saw him outside," I said. "Jac's mom had just kidnapped her. I was still standing there with Max on the sidewalk. And Orin came out of the house. I'd kind of wondered who you were in your office with."

She nodded.

"So he introduced himself and stuff. Then he went to get his bike. And I decided to go back in the van Hechts' — in the house next door."

"Go back?"

I sighed.

"I *am* doing my BC project on the house. I didn't make that up. I was over there photographing yesterday, and the screen door was easy to open. A window was propped up. So I went in."

I hesitated. Trying to decide how much I should tell her.

"But I've been getting these ... kind of spells, recently. Around spirits. I got really freaked out in the house. One of the spirits in there is very strong, and very angry. It was doing everything it could to get my attention. The more I tried to ignore it, the more forceful it got. I lost it — started screaming bloody murder. Orin heard me, and came in to help."

Again, I found myself presenting only part of the truth to my mother. It was so humiliating.

"Orin told me I was having panic attacks. He said . . . he showed me how to do breathing and stuff. He said he could teach me . . . other ways. To, like, manage my energy or something. He said I'd overloaded my system, and that was causing the panic attacks."

My mom sat, nodding a little, and waiting. She gave me an encouraging smile.

"I'm sorry — I shouldn't have tried to pretend like I hadn't met Orin. It's just all so complicated. But I thought if I told you about him, I'd have to tell you about the panic attacks and the . . . I just don't want to talk about it. About me. I'm so sick of me right now." I made a noise of frustration.

"But you seem angry at me," my mother said.

I didn't say anything. Because the fact was, I did feel angry with my mother. And if

I admitted that, she'd want to know what she had done. And I knew very well she hadn't done anything wrong. All she had done was to continue being herself.

"I can't — I just can't talk about this with you. I'm not even making any sense."

"No, you make perfect sense, Kat," she said. She reached over to pick up my mug and took a sip of tea.

"Your intuition is telling you not to come to me for guidance right now," she continued. "You have to honor that, Kat. You're right to honor that. Coming into the sight is different for every single person. It's never the same experience twice. And in the end, all you have is your intuition. Intuition is a line to your higher spirit. The part of you that's multi-dimensional, that has access to unlimited knowledge and help. You've got to go where that takes you. Maybe the Universe brought Orin to you today, instead of guiding you to me."

"I don't understand," I said.

"Things always happen for a reason. When you watch a movie, and the main character has a random encounter with someone, you know that encounter has meaning. That it's important to the story, or it wouldn't be in the movie. Real life is the same way."

She got up and went over to the counter near the telephone, and came back with a card in her hand.

"This is Orin's card," she said, handing it to me. "His phone number and his e-mail address are there. If you feel the impulse to contact him about something, do it."

I took the card. It said ORIN WATKINS — HEALING AND ENERGY WORK in plain letters.

Below were a phone number, a Web site, and an e-mail address.

"You're going to be okay, Kat," my mom said, reaching over and pushing the hair out of my eyes. "I trust you. Trust your-self, okay?"

If only it were that easy.

I put Orin's card in my desk drawer. I e-mailed Jac a few times, telling her all about Orin and how he'd rescued me in the house. I got no response, though. Jac's mom was probably keeping her off the computer, or maybe she'd even taken her somewhere. So I'd be getting no advice from my best friend. I sat, my mind blank. Then an idea came to me out of the blue.

"That's stupid," I thought.

But where had the idea come from? Maybe it was more of that intuition my mother was talking about.

I Googled Philips Memorial Hospital and got their phone number. I dialed it.

"Philips Memorial, how may I help you?"

I had intended to ask if Julius van Hecht was still a patient there. But it came to me suddenly that if I was entitled to any information about Julius, I would know that.

"Uh, yes, can you tell me the room number for Julius van Hecht, please? I've misplaced it."

There was a pause, and I thought the woman was going to tell me to buzz off. But in a moment she came back on the line.

"Room seven sixteen," she said.

I took a quick breath of surprise.

"Uh, thanks," I said, and hung up.

Julius was still alive, and he was still in the same hospital.

Twenty minutes later, I was on the bus. Philips Memorial wasn't that close. I'd have to transfer twice — the trip there would probably take forty-five minutes, give or take. With my mother giving me my space and Jac virtually locked up in her own home, I'd had nobody to bounce the idea off of. Which left me with two choices: forget about the whole thing or just do it. Here I was on the bus, just doing it.

I had no idea what I was going to do when I got to the hospital. I just felt like I needed to see Julius. That somehow by seeing Julius, I'd find out more about Tank's mystery. My mother says that sometimes we just need to take action and trust the Universe to handle the details. There seemed like a lot of details here even for the Universe, but the sad fact was, this was the only plan I had.

The third bus let me off right outside the hospital. Philips Memorial was a mid-sized hospital, situated on top of a ridge that looked over the surrounding valleys. As I walked up the paved pathway toward the front entrance, I heard an ambulance siren scream by, and I felt a chill. I didn't like hospitals. I mean, who did? But I had a special thing about them. Whenever we drove by a hospital, I'd fix my gaze on a particular window, knowing that there was a patient behind it. Maybe sleeping. Or being operated on. Or dying. I did the same thing when an ambulance went by. I'd try to get my head around the reality that there was a person in that ambulance. Someone sick, or injured. And I'd never know who they were, or what happened to them.

I walked through the main entrance of the hospital into a sunny lobby. There was a desk by the elevators, where a dour-looking middle-aged woman sat.

"Room number?" she asked.

"Excuse me?"

"What room are you visiting?" the woman said. She looked at me like I was the stupidest person she'd seen so far that day.

"Oh, sorry. Um, room seven sixteen."

The woman fished a card that said 7 1 6 on it from a file. She pushed a clipboard toward me.

"Sign here," she said.

I signed my name, my real one, since I hadn't thought to come up with a fake name and didn't want to stand around wondering what to write. It probably didn't matter. Always better to be honest. And in fact, I hadn't actually done anything wrong. I was just going to visit a patient, nothing more.

The woman directed me to a bank of elevators. There was one waiting there, and I was relieved to find I was the only passenger. I had gone to a hospital a few years back, to visit a classmate who had broken her leg. There had been a man on a gurney with me in the elevator, along with a nurse. The man had made strange, unhappy sounds in his throat, while the nurse chatted to a doctor about some restaurant like the guy wasn't lying right there. I couldn't have gotten off that elevator any faster.

The seventh floor seemed unusually quiet and empty. I followed the room numbers down the hall. Room 716 was directly opposite the nurse's station, but there was no one there. Relieved, I walked quickly to the room. The door was open, and I peeked inside. I caught a quick glimpse of a figure standing by the window, then hurriedly stepped away from the doorway.

A nurse was coming down the hall toward the nurse's station. I knew it must look strange, the way I was standing there a few feet from the doorway. She gave me a curious look, then peered into Julius's room.

"Leaving so soon?" she called into the room.

I took off down the hall. Whoever was visiting Julius was about to come out of the room, and I didn't want to be seen. I darted into the bathroom and locked the door. I checked my watch and waited. I pressed my ear against the door, but I couldn't hear anything other than regular hospital sounds.

After about five minutes, I ventured out. There was an older couple standing near the water fountain, talking to a doctor. The nurse was at her station. And the door to 716 was still open. I decided to walk past the room, glance in to see if the visitor had gone, then pretend I had accidentally walked too far.

I'm sure if the nurse had been watching me, my acting would have looked pathetic. I had seen that the room was empty, then gone to the next room, and made a big show of looking at that room number, then examining my Room 716 visitor's card. Stupid. But the nurse was on the phone and typing something on her computer at the same time. I darted into 716.

Julius was lying in the room's only bed, positioned by the window. From where I stood, he looked like he was asleep. But when

I got closer, I could see his eyes were partly opened. A machine nearby was beeping slowly. That was the only sound in the room. The walls were decorated with drawings and cards. On the wall opposite the bed, a painting was taped to the wall — I immediately recognized it as the same sunburst I'd seen in Tank's bedroom. If Julius were to open his eyes, it would be the first thing he'd see.

I stood near the bed, feeling guilty and ashamed like I was violating the boy's privacy. Even though he was in a coma, it seemed rude to just stand there looking at him without saying anything. He wasn't a museum exhibit. He was a person.

"Hi," I said quietly. "I'm Kat. I live next door to you . . . I mean, I live next door to your house. On Seth Avenue."

Julius's chest rose and fell. His dark,

straight hair had been neatly cut short. Though he was very thin, he didn't look particularly sick. I guessed from looking at him that he was about my age.

"I'm really sorry about what happened to you," I said. "Nobody deserves that."

The sound of Julius's breathing, punctuated by the slow blip of the machine, was strangely soothing. Something about it reminded me of a foghorn.

"But don't give up hope, Julius. You could still wake up and be fine. It happens. Seriously. I've read about times where . . . about cases in which someone is asleep for years and then they just wake up. It could happen to you, too, Julius. You're still a kid, and everything. You've just, like, missed a whole bunch of school. Which is not necessarily a bad thing."

Julius's eyes were completely closed now. He would be cute, I thought, if he weren't so thin. If he weren't in a coma.

"I guess it's pretty weird that I'm here, right? I mean, we didn't know each other or anything. Before. I moved next door to your house later. After your family . . ."

It occurred to me that Julius might not know his family had moved. They say a person in a coma can sometimes understand what is being said. I didn't want to upset him.

"I mean, after your accident. I moved in a few months or so after that happened. So we never met. I just kind of needed to see you. It's hard to explain, really. It's actually because of your brother that I'm here. I saw him, and I got this strong feeling that for some reason he wanted me to come here.

That's what this is all really about — it's because of Tank. It's what Tank needed."

As soon as I mentioned Tank's name, Julius's eyes moved under his eyelids, the way people do when they're dreaming. The machine began to beep faster.

"I . . . what is it, Julius? Is it about Tank? Is there something important I need to know about Tank?"

The machine beeped a little faster. Julius's eyes kept moving around, and his lip began to twitch. It was really freaking me out.

I had upset him. The sound of Tank's name seemed to have really agitated Julius. I was scared and ashamed at the same time.

"I'm sorry, Julius. I didn't mean to upset you. I'm going to go now."

I walked quickly out of the room and stood in the hallway, leaning my head against the wall. My heart was beating hard and I was beginning to feel the now familiar sensations of a panic attack. But why now? Why here?

Because you're in a hospital, *stupid,* I told myself. There are probably dead people all over the place. And now they're trying to get your attention.

I felt the blood rush to my face, and I started doing the breathing Orin had taught me.

Soooo, hum. Soooo, hum.

Orin had said he could teach me how to manage my energy — how to separate myself from spirits without sending my body into meltdown. Why hadn't I just asked him to tell me right then? At the moment, it seemed like the most important information in the world. Too bad I didn't have it.

I stood perfectly still, trying to shut out everything but the sound of my breath and the words *so* and *hum*. Slowly, I started to feel a little more normal.

"Are you okay, honey?"

I turned around, carefully, because I was still a little dizzy. It was the nurse from the station, standing next to me. Her large, brown eyes seemed concerned and kind.

"Oh, yeah. No, I'm fine. I was just ... taking some breaths, you know?"

"Sure, sweetie," the nurse said, smiling. Her name tag said RITA LEIGH. "Amazing how often people forget to breathe."

I nodded, then swallowed.

"Just in for a visit?"

I looked down at my hands, clutching the big card that said 7 1 6. So it was obvious I'd been in Julius's room.

"Um, yeah," I said, nodding and making that pained, sympathetic face that goes along with visiting the sick.

"How's my guy doing today?" Rita asked.

"Oh, well, you know. Fine. I mean, I guess he's about the same."

Rita nodded, wrinkling her brow slightly.

"Yeah. He gets taken care of real good, that's for sure. His mama is here every day, for hours at a time. Reading to him, and brushing his hair and massaging his muscles. But you probably know that. I haven't seen you before, though."

"Oh, no," I said quickly. "I didn't . . . I mean, I haven't visited that much. I just . . . you know, I get to thinking about the accident sometimes, and I want to pop by and see how he's doing. People wake up from comas, don't they?"

"They do, sometimes," Rita said. "When you've been down more than two years, it's not so common. But it does happen."

"So it's possible. Julius could wake up," I said.

"Julius?" Rita asked. She seemed to give me a funny look.

Uh oh. What had I said wrong? Julius van Hecht was listed as room 7 1 6, and that was the room I went into. Had I made a mistake? Could there be more than one kid in a coma at Philips Memorial?

"I'm sorry?" I asked.

"Nobody ever calls him Julius," Rita said. "I guess you don't know him that well."

Uh oh.

"Yeah, no," I said, looking at my feet, then back into Rita's wide brown eyes. She didn't look angry, or suspicious. Just curious.

"The truth is I barely know him at all. I'm from his neighborhood — our house is next door to where he lived when it happened . . . and I just . . ."

Rita nodded.

"No, I understand, sweetie. Sometimes we feel connected to a person after something like this happens, even if we weren't connected before. I'm glad you came by. Tank needs all the visitors he can get."

My mouth dropped open.

"Tank?"

Rita laughed.

"Yep. That's what folks who know him call him. His whole name is Julius Sherman van Hecht, and his mom said he hated the Julius part, and he wasn't much keener on the Sherman part. But Sherman is also the name of a kind of tank — did you know that? And he loved playing with toy tanks ever since he was in diapers. So they call him Tank."

My panic attack was coming back.

"I need to go," I said, backing away.

"Are you sure you're okay, sweetie? I could get you some water."

"Thanks, I'm fine," I called over my shoulder. If I was going to pass out again, I'd rather be in the elevator where I had the chance of doing so privately.

The elevator came almost immediately. This time, there was a man already in it. He took no notice of me. He just stared at his shoes, his eyes blank. I stood in the corner, holding on to the railing and doing Orin's breathing. A million thoughts were trying to bust into my mind, and I struggled to keep them out.

I had seen Tank's spirit in the house. A young Tank. About the age he'd been before the accident.

But Tank wasn't dead.

What had I seen? What was happening to me?

When we came to the lobby, I sprinted for the door. I guess I heard someone calling, but I didn't think they were talking to me. I was halfway through the door when I felt a hand on my shoulder. It scared me so much I let out a shriek.

"Excuse me!" It was the dour woman from the front desk. "I did call out to you, several times."

My heart *thunk-thunk*ed in my chest. What was going on? Had Rita called down to the desk? Should I just make a break for it? But I felt too dizzy and disoriented to run anywhere.

"The card, young lady. You need to give it back," the woman said. She sounded kinder now, probably because I looked so freaked out.

I was clutching the 7 1 6 card so hard I'd crumpled it. I handed it back to her.

"Sorry," I mumbled.

"Quite alright," she said. "Hospital policy — you are issued the card when you go up, and you return it when you leave. And you'll need to sign out as well."

"Sure, yeah," I said. I meekly followed her back to the front desk. She pushed the clipboard toward me, and I picked up the pen and signed my name and departure time. I glanced up at the many other signatures on the page, and my eye fell on a familiar number. 716. I looked over at the signature column to see who else had been in to visit Tank today.

The signature read *Orin Watkins.*

Chapter 12

That evening I tried to do some work on my BC project, but I just couldn't concentrate. I kept running the details of my day over and over in my head. What I really needed was to call Jac, but her mother was *not* being cool about me calling. I gave up after a few tries, half convinced that Jac wasn't even getting my messages.

Hoping she might be checking her e-mail, if they hadn't taken her computer away, I shot off one asking her to call me

ASAP. I was surprised when my phone rang just a few minutes after sending the e-mail.

"That was fast! Are you going to get in trouble for calling me? What if your mom tries to use the phone?"

"I've repossessed my cell phone," Jac said. Her voice sounded slightly muffled, like she was surrounded by towels or something. "I left the case in my mother's drawer where she put it. Hopefully she won't notice."

"You sound like you're in a closet," I said.

"Easily explained, Sherlock. I *am* in the closet. And I've got Yo-Yo Ma playing the Dvořák Cello Concerto in B minor on my CD player. The closet should muffle the sound of my voice, and Mommy Dearest will probably think my listening to Yo-Yo Ma is the first step in my cello recovery. Maybe she'll even leave me alone for a minute. So what's up?"

"I went to the hospital today."

"Oh no, what happened? Are you okay?" Jac asked anxiously.

"No, I'm fine, Jac. I went to the hospital where Julius is. I had to see him with my own eyes. He was my only link to Tank. So I went to his room."

"No. You. Did. Not."

"I did. I just walked right in. It was no problem."

I left out the bit about the close call with the other visitor and the nurse, because I wasn't sure how much time Jac had on the phone. Somehow I wasn't as convinced as she was that her mother wouldn't come poking around in her room for no good reason.

"Julius is Tank, Jac."

"Say what?"

"Julius and Tank aren't brothers. They're the same person. It's a nickname. Tank is alive."

There was a long pause. I could hear Yo-Yo Ma playing enthusiastically in the background.

"Okay, I'm confused, Voodoo Mama. If Tank is alive, then how could he . . . how could you . . ."

"I know. How could I see the ghost of a living person? I've been running it over and over in my head, Jac. The only thing I can think of is that because Tank is in a coma, his consciousness has somehow gotten out of his body and is able to move around. Kind of."

"But how . . . isn't . . ."

"I'm just guessing, remember. But I had this dream, Jac, where Tank was in a boat that was attached to the shore by a cord. And I was trying to get to him. But then the cord was cut, and he began to drift away. See?"

"Merrily merrily merrily merrily, life is but a dream?" Jac asked.

"No. I think the boat represented Tank's consciousness — his spirit. The dream was explaining why Tank needed help. His spirit is in danger of separating from his body. My mom says that our spirits are connected to our bodies by a silver cord of energy. If that cord gets cut, Tank's spirit might not be able to find its way back to his body. And if the spirit stays out of a living body too long, it might not ever be able to find its way back. Maybe that's why he won't wake up."

"Whoa."

"I know, right?" I said, grinning. "But it's the best theory I can come up with. And my . . . my intuition tells me I'm on the right track."

"Okay, so let's say you're right. How do you help Tank?"

I sighed.

"I haven't the slightest idea," I said. "I know how to contact the dead, not to reconnect the living with their bodies."

"Well, what does your famous intuition say?"

I sighed again, deeper this time.

"I'm coming up empty except for one option, which I'm not crazy about."

"Spit it out, Voodoo Mama."

"When I was leaving the hospital, I had to sign out. And I noticed that Tank had had another visitor just before me. Orin Watkins."

"Shaggy hot guy you told me about?" Jac exclaimed.

My cheeks flushed, and I was glad she couldn't see me.

"Yeah. It's crazy, right? But he's obviously connected to Tank. Remember, the first time I saw him he was standing outside Tank's house, just staring at it. Now he's been to see Tank in the hospital. I'm at a dead end here, no pun intended, and it seems like Orin is the only person who might know what to do next."

"Okay, so what's the problem?" Jac asked.

Just that asking for his help is the last thing I want to do, I thought. Maybe it was simply because Orin was a guy. A strange, older, more or less hot guy. Or it might have been because he was my mom's friend. A good-looking friend with similar interests. And how was that a problem? I wasn't sure. But the very idea of Orin made me feel uncomfortable, the kind of discomfort when you suddenly remember something you forgot to do.

"I just don't know him very well, Jac. It's weird. The whole thing makes me kind of uncomfortable."

"Mmm," Jac said. "Doesn't sound like you have much of a choice, though, if you want to help Tank."

I frowned. I *did* want to help Tank. He was on my mind constantly. I was beginning to think I felt part of his consciousness hovering around me, very faintly. Like a butterfly.

"Shoot, gotta hop. E-mail me, bye!"

The line went dead. I hoped Jac had not just been pulled out of the closet by her mother. I sent her another e-mail, asking if she was okay. Then I climbed into bed and lay there for a long time, staring at the ceiling.

The next morning, I was awakened by the sound of my mother singing downstairs. I got up, put on my robe, and picked up Orin's card from my desk. I grabbed my cell phone, started to dial his number, then snapped the phone shut. I stared at the phone glumly, then opened it and dialed Jac's cell phone number. I'd been dialing it periodically since Jac's mother had taken her away, and it always went straight to voicemail. But this time, it rang.

"Do *not* ask me how I am," I heard.

"Jac?"

"This is Jac if you agree not to ask me how I am," she said.

"I'm just glad I got you," I said. "I've been worried about you. Did your mom catch you?"

"Sort of," Jac replied. "She caught me in the closet. But I had time to stash the phone in a boot. I told her I could only listen to Yo-Yo Ma in an extremely enclosed and safe place."

"Mmmm. Did she buy it?"

"Not likely. But there was no evidence that I was in the closet for any evil reason, so she dropped it. But she's all over me now, constantly barging into my room. A girl could get a complex."

"Is it okay that you're on the phone now?"

"Oh it's fine. Even Mommy Dearest has to leave the house sometimes. She's having her hideous helmet hair varnished, or whatever they do down at her salon. Then she's taking her car for a tune-up. I'm good for at least two hours. And like I said, I don't want to talk about *her.*"

You just did, I thought, but I was wise enough to keep it to myself.

"Okay. So I thought it over last night, and I think I'm going to call Orin."

"Good," Jac said. "Do you know how to get in touch with him?"

"My mom gave me his card. She said he'd be a good person to go to for help about . . . the kind of stuff I might be having problems with, if I couldn't confide in her. But I feel weird about it."

"Well, presumably if your mom gave you his card, she feels comfortable about him — like he's not an axe murder or anything. Obviously your mom thinks highly of him, or she'd never have encouraged you to go to him. That's a *good* thing, Kat, that she likes him. Or is that the problem? Are you afraid Orin might be stepfather material?"

I opened my mouth to say "Of course not!" but nothing came out. I hadn't actually realized it 'til Jac said it out loud, but she'd pinpointed why Orin made me uncomfortable. He seemed sort of cool, and he definitely had things to teach me, but I was afraid if he were around more, Orin and my mom might end up getting involved, which opened up a can of worms that confused me, grossed me out, and riled me up in all sorts of ways.

"If we can't talk about *your* mother, then I don't think we should talk about mine either," I said, a tad defensively.

"I wasn't exactly talking about her, but I get your drift. But Orin's not your mother, so let's talk about him."

I squirmed and said nothing.

"I agree with your intuition. You need to get in touch with Orin so you can figure out the Tank thing. Maybe he knows things about Tank that you don't. And vice versa. I think you guys should join forces."

"Yeah, I know, but I still feel weird about it. Calling some . . . man. It just feels . . . I mean, just because my mother trusts him . . . I'll need to get to know him better before I can judge him."

"I think what you're saying is you don't mind getting his help, but you feel weird or embarrassed to be alone with him."

"Yeah," I mumbled.

"So see if he can meet you somewhere public. And I'll go with you. Because then you'll be comfortable, plus if I don't get out of this house I'm going to strangle myself."

"What about your —"

"Uh uh uh!" Jac warned.

No mother talk.

"You can get away?" I asked.

"My mother can't possibly get home for at least two hours. Probably more like two and a half. Look, it's . . . nine fifteen now. Try and get ahold of this guy, and figure out a place to meet, then call and tell me where."

"Jac, you're in so much trouble already. Do you really think it's a good idea to sneak out again?"

"I think it's the best. Idea. Ever." Jac declared. "You know what? I'm leaving the house anyway. Orin or no Orin. I need some cake. So don't put this guilt trip on yourself that I'm going to get in trouble because of you. Trust me, I plan on getting in trouble no matter what. Call him now, okay, Kat?"

I sighed.

"Okay."

Jac hung up without saying good-bye, which she often does when she's ready to move on with the next segment of her day. I picked up Orin's card again, stared at it for a moment, then dialed.

Chapter 13

Orin didn't sound at all surprised to hear from me. Maybe he had a touch of clairvoyance, or else he was just one of those people who played it cool. Either way, he acted like he'd been expecting my call.

"So I take it you're ready to start learning about energy? We can start with how to manage all the spirits trying to get your attention, but you're going to need a basic education in the property of psychic energy, too."

"No, Orin, I don't . . . I mean, yes, I would

like to learn about that stuff. The panic attacks aren't going away by themselves or anything. But this isn't about that."

"Okay," Orin said, sort of carefully.

I decided there was no point in a cloak-and-dagger routine. I cut to the chase.

"I'm calling because of Tank."

There was a pause.

"Tank? I'm sorry, Kat, but you're taking me by surprise. Did you know him? I thought you moved to Seth Avenue after . . . after."

"We did," I said. "It's complicated. Um, okay, those panic attacks I've been having? That you said are from me blocking spirits trying to get my attention? It all started inside that house next door. Tank's house. There's a reason I keep going back to that house even though there's an old man there who terrorized me. It's because I saw something. I saw Tank, well, Tank from before the accident, for the first time a couple days ago. Ever since then, I've felt like —"

"Wait," Orin said. "You *saw* Tank?"

I nodded, then remembered I was on the phone and Orin couldn't see me.

"Yeah," I replied.

"Where was he? What happened?"

"From my room, I can see his window. I was thinking about doing a photography project on the house, because it seemed like it had a lot of stories to tell. And I saw Tank — actually I accidentally photographed him. That's what gave me the idea to go over there the first time. I found his room. It has this sunburst painted on it."

"Kat, this is important. Did you make contact with Tank? Was he able to communicate with you?"

"Well, that's the thing," I said. "I couldn't. He didn't seem to see me or know I was there at all. Listen, I'm confused, Orin. How do *you* know Tank? And if Tank's alive, who did I see over there? Is it possible his consciousness is traveling while he's in a coma?"

"Kat, are you willing to go back over to the van Hecht house? I'd like to meet you there."

I paused. The whole reason I'd called Orin was to suggest we meet. But I wasn't sure if I was ready to go back to the van Hecht house, where I was so likely to face the enraged old man again.

"I know it was scary the last time you were there, Kat. I know there's a particular spirit who's causing you a great deal of stress. But I think you might need to face it in order to get past your problem. And in doing so, you may be the only person who can help me with mine."

There was another silence.

"Oh man, what am I thinking?" Orin said suddenly. "I'm not thinking, that's the problem. This must sound . . . Kat, you're right to be cautious. You don't know me and you don't trust me, and that's smart of you. You shouldn't be meeting me alone in an abandoned house. I'm sure if you ask, your mother would come along. That way, you'd feel safe."

This was exactly what I did not want — my mother coming along to meet Orin in an old house.

"No," I said hastily. "I trust you. My mom gave me your card, actually, so . . . I mean, it's okay, anyway. My friend Jac will be with me. I'll meet you on the van Hecht's back porch in an hour, okay?"

"Well —"

"An hour, okay?" I repeated.

Orin said okay, and I hung up before he could bring my mother up again. I walked to the window and stared out at the van Hecht house.

I turned away from the window, picked up my phone, and dialed Jac's number.

Rather than explain Jac's presence to my mother, which would probably involve more lying, I told Jac to go straight around the back of the van Hecht house to the porch. I wasn't expecting her to beat me there, so when she said hello as I was opening the porch door, I squealed.

"Ha! Scaredy Kat."

"Oh, stop. You'd scream, too, if I jumped

out of the shadows at you," I grumbled, opening the porch door and going in.

"I didn't jump out of anything," Jac said cheerfully. "I didn't move a muscle. I said 'hiya,' and you made a sound like a kitten on a roller coaster. A biiiiiiig kitten with a healthy pair of lungs."

I stuck my tongue out at her. Then I gestured toward the kitchen.

"The last time I was here, Jac, every cabinet door in that kitchen banged open and shut by itself."

Jac paused to consider this, peering in through the window.

"Cool," she said.

I was tempted to tell Jac I saw a bee. That would plant the ball of terror firmly in her court. But I resisted the urge.

"So, are you okay?" I asked.

Jac gave me a sideways look, then got up and rehung the wind chimes, brushing her fingers through them and making them sound lightly.

"Not really," Jac said.

"What can I do?" I asked. I studied her little face in profile, her red hair clipped short to reveal tiny ears, and her upturned nose looking especially elfin today. She looked tired.

"Just this," Jac replied, sweeping her hand toward the interior of the van Hecht house. "Be your unpredictable explosive supernatural self. Call me to come along on your adventures. Help me to forget about the cello, and about . . . her. It's such a relief not to have to be that version of me, even if it's just for a while. I hope we run into a whole team of vampires in there, Kat. Seriously. The freakier, the better."

I smiled.

"Happy to be of service," I said. "And welcome to Kat's House of Terror."

Jac grinned.

"Now all we need is your hottie healer friend. Where is he, anyway?"

"I'm right here," came a deep voice.

Jac and I both jumped. The screen door opened.

"Hi," Orin said. "Sorry if I'm late."

I shook my head.

"You're not late," I mumbled. "Um, this is my friend Jac."

"Pleased to meet you," Orin said. Then he grinned.

Had he heard Jac call him the "hottie healer"? He must have. My face was burning, and I was sure it was flushed a bright red.

"Well, are we ready to go in?" Orin asked. His face was more or less expressionless, but to me he seemed amused. I felt my cheeks go even redder.

"I'm ready," Jac said eagerly.

"Me, too," I said quietly. Anything to get my bright red face pointing in another direction. Yikes.

"Just one thing first," Orin said.

I froze. *Please don't let him comment about the hottie thing*, I prayed.

"Kat," Orin said.

I'd been staring in the opposite direction to hide my face, but I had no choice but to turn toward him.

"Close your eyes for a minute."

Okay, that was weird. But I did it.

"I want you to visualize the stream of energy inside you. It starts at your feet and rises through your body like a river of light, moving all the time."

I'd done basic energy meditations with my mother, so this wasn't too far out of left field.

"Okay," I said.

"Now imagine that energy is coming out of the top of your head, and flowing down around you before going back into your feet. It's completely encasing you in a bubble."

"Okay," I said after a moment. I wasn't stringing him along. I could feel the energy rushing through me. It made a whooshing feeling in my stomach, like I was on a roller coaster.

"This bubble will protect you, Kat. Nothing can penetrate it unless you invite it in. Everything else will stay outside of the bubble. Nothing can approach you unless you specifically ask it to. Understand?"

I nodded.

"Let's go then," Orin said.

When we walked into the kitchen all was quiet, but I still felt creeped out by the memory of all those banging doors. I shivered slightly and closed my eyes to see if I could sense the presence of anything in the room. Orin must have noticed what I was doing.

"Don't," Orin said. "That's as good as an invitation. This is only about Tank right now. Focus only on him, and the other spirits will be kept out."

I nodded.

"Okay. Let's go upstairs."

Orin went first. I followed, and Jac brought up the rear. The house was dead silent. No chairs scraping across the floor. No rolling balls. No thuds. The only sound was the creak of the stairs as we ascended them.

When we reached the top of the stairs, I

pushed past Orin and walked to the doorway of Tank's room. I wasn't afraid at all at the moment. Tank never scared me, and Orin's energy bubble made me feel safe. I peered into the room.

And there he was, in the same place I'd seen him before. He was sitting on the floor, his head resting on the wide windowsill that faced my room. He looked like he was sleeping.

"Are we going in?" came Jac's voice from behind me.

"What is it, Kat? Do you see him?" asked Orin, more quietly.

I walked inside and stepped to one side to make room for them to come in.

"He's there," I said softly, pointing toward the window.

"Where?" asked Jac.

"Try to talk to him," said Orin.

I took several steps in Tank's direction.

"Tank? Tank, it's me, Kat. Remember? I live next door."

I was close enough to him now to see that his eyes weren't closed. His head rested on his arms, and he stared out the window.

I changed my tactic. Instead of speaking to Tank, I closed my eyes and imagined my satellite dish scanning the sky. I said Tank's name to myself, indicating that I was searching only for Tank's spirit. I didn't pick up anything. I could see Tank clearly, right in front of me. But I sensed nothing. Or less than nothing. My tuner wasn't picking up static — it was picking up an overwhelming lack of anything. Like a black hole. He was there, but he wasn't there.

"What's going on?" Jac whispered. "Is there a ghost in here right now?"

"It's not working," I said, turning to Orin.

He was staring at the place by the window with an intense look of concentration.

"Do you see him?" I asked.

"Is that where the ghost is?" Jac asked eagerly. I shot her a look.

"No," replied Orin. "But because you've told me he's there, I can pick up some energy. Not something I would have noticed on my own. But I know now that I'm picking up something from Tank. I'm just not able to work with it."

Jac walked over to the painting of the sunburst and stared at it, transfixed. I was glad she was momentarily distracted.

"Kat," Orin said suddenly. "Neither of us can interact with Tank on our own. But I think if we work together, it might make a difference. Do you trust me?"

I nodded. For whatever reason, I did trust

Orin implicitly. And my intuition had always been good.

"All right. I'm going to do some energy work right now, on both of us. I'm going to try to sync up our vibratory fields, and at the same time I'm going to try to establish an energetic link between our fifth chakras."

I wanted to ask him if it would hurt, but I just nodded. I watched Tank while Orin closed his eyes and began deep breathing. I wondered what Tank was looking at through that window — or if he saw anything at all.

Then I closed my eyes, not because Orin told me to, but because I knew it would help. I could feel the energy shift almost immediately. I saw waves and swirls of violet light. The whooshing feeling in my stomach intensified. I felt a spreading warmth in my chest and throat, like a warm liquid was seeping over and through me.

This is amazing, I thought. *Orin is the real deal.* I had never studied energy, but I recognized what I was feeling. Orin was changing the level and type of energy in me. He was activating something. My senses were heightened, and there were huge waves of energy passing through me.

"Kat?"

His voice sounded like it was coming from a million miles away.

I tried to say something back.

"We need to try and contact him now," Orin said.

"How?" I murmured.

"Try speaking to him again."

It was a huge effort just to open my eyes. I felt like I was in a deep sleep, and I was incredibly comfortable. The last thing in the world I wanted to do was wake up. Somehow, I managed to open my eyes.

"Tank?" I said sleepily.

It could have been my imagination, but Tank seemed to startle at the sound of his name.

"Tank," I repeated. "I'm here. I'm . . . I'm your friend. I'm here to help you. Do you see me, Tank?"

And he turned his face and looked directly at me.

"He's looking at me," I whispered to Orin.

"Tell him you can help him if he listens to you carefully."

I repeated Orin's words to Tank. His eyes widened slightly.

"Tell him that he's been in an accident, and that his body is in a coma. Tell him his consciousness has separated from his body, and it needs to return. We'll help him find his way back. It may help him to wake up."

I did, masking my surprise. Could we really do that? Is that what Orin had been trying to do all along — wake Tank up?

Orin murmured the words and I repeated them to Tank.

"Envision a pillar of light in front of you. Reach out and put your hands into the pillar. Now step into the pillar. The light is coming out from the top of your head. It runs through your body. It leaves your feet and continues into the earth. Bathe in this light. Let it soak into every cell, every organ in your body. This is the light of divine healing. Accept the light. Accept the healing."

Tank's face was upturned, his eyes wide and eager.

"Now tell Tank to look down at his

midsection. He will see a silver cord of light coming out of him."

I told Tank this. Though I saw no cord, Tank's hands flew to something near his ribs. His hands wrapped around something invisible.

Orin continued to whisper instructions.

"Now, Tank, follow this cord. This is the cord that connects you to your physical body. When you reach the end of the cord, you will have come home to your physical self. When you are in your body, recall the divine healing light again. This will seal your life force back into your physical form."

Tank was reaching out and pulling his hands in toward his chest one at a time. It was as if he was holding a rope and guiding something at the end of it closer in. He pulled and pulled, like a fisherman hauling in a net. Then suddenly he stopped. He looked surprised, and confused. He turned and looked straight at me. I nodded encouragement.

"It's okay," I said. "It's okay, Tank."

He cocked his head to one side like a puppy, then turned back toward the cord.

And then he disappeared.

Chapter 14

"Are you sure your phone is charged?" Jac asked for the third time.

We were at our old table at the Bean Factory. We each had an extra tall Mocha-Cho. Jac also had a brick-sized cake-like concoction called a Chocolate Rocket Loaf. It looked like a Twinkie on steroids.

Orin had gone to the hospital to check on Tank. He was supposed to call when he had news. We had also told him where he could find us, if he needed to. As we were leaving the van Hecht house (Jac somewhat reluctantly, because she had witnessed nothing supernatural at all), Orin explained that the van Hechts had hired him a year ago. Tank's mother had gone to a healing convention and met Orin there. She was skeptical of the whole "healer" thing, but she was also desperate.

Tank had recovered from his injuries, and his body and brain were strong and healthy. No doctor could offer any advice or measure of hope as to whether or not Tank would ever wake up. Unwilling to give up, they turned to Orin for help. He had visited Tank frequently, working with him in the hospital room, but he had found, as I did, that there was a disconnect. Tank's body was there, but the energy work did nothing. Then, after dreaming about the sunburst painting, Orin had started biking past the van Hecht house, sensing Tank was strongly connected there. And that's when I came into the picture.

"He's really cute, Kat. Seriously."

I glanced up at Jac, part startled, part embarrassed.

"What? Oh man, Kat. Are you crushing on the hottie healer?"

I made an explosive sound of irritation.

"What?" Jac repeated, a little too innocently.

"Drop it, okay?" I muttered.

Jac watched me carefully, but she didn't say anything else for a while.

I slurped sulkily on my Mocha-Cho.

"I'm sorry," Jac said finally. "I meant that as a joke. I mean, I thought it would be funny. Maybe it isn't funny."

I looked up at her. The teasing air had left her. She did look sorry.

"I'm not crushing on him," I said. "Not

really. I don't know, maybe a tiny bit. I mean, obviously he's really cute. But he's also . . . you know, he's the real deal. What he did back there in the van Hecht's house — that energy stuff — it was really something."

"Yeah," Jac said, a tad dreamily. "So is it because of your mom?"

I studied Jac for a moment. She took a huge bite of the Chocolate Rocket Loaf. It looked like she unhinged her jaw to open her mouth wide enough.

"Since my dad left a couple years ago, it's been just us," I said.

Jac knew the basic facts behind my father's departure. She nodded, chewed, and waited for me to continue. She had a little smudge of chocolate in each corner of her mouth.

"When there are three of you, then suddenly there are two of you, you can get really tight with a person. You know, he didn't just leave her, and he didn't just leave me. He left both of us. We had all this solidarity, right? Like we'd show him. We'd be happier, just the two of us on our own, than we had been with him in the picture."

Jac nodded again.

"I'm not saying I want it to stay that way forever. I'm not saying I don't ever want my mom to meet somebody, or be happy. I'm not."

I stabbed at my Mocha-Cho with the straw.

"I'm just not sure I'm ready for it now, I guess. I don't know at what point in time I would be happy if my mother found some guy she wanted to date. Definitely it's okay in theory. I'm just not ready for it today. Not today. Not tomorrow. That's all I know."

The straw made a squeaking noise as I

continued poking at the bottom of the Mocha-Cho cup.

"And it's always been fine because it's never been a reality. And then Orin comes along, and he knows so much. He's intuitive, and he's got this gift. And okay. Yeah. He's gorgeous. And he offers to teach me stuff about working with energy that would really help me deal with seeing spirits."

Jac broke the rest of the Chocolate Rocket Loaf into two pieces, then four. Her eyes never left mine.

"But I'm resisting it. Because then he might be around. And you know ... he's a healer, she's a medium. They're already friends. Why wouldn't they be into each other? I just don't think I could handle that. But then I think, man, I'm so selfish! Who am I to keep them apart just because it's what I want?"

Jac pushed a hunk of chocolate loaf in my direction.

"Okay, Kat, wait a second. I can totally understand your feeling weird about the possibility that one day your mom might date somebody, even Orin. Especially Orin. It's fine for you to feel that way. It's normal. She's your mom!

"You think she doesn't have weird feelings about *you* dating a boy someday? I guarantee you she does, even if she wants you to be happy and even if she wants you to have a boyfriend."

I took a bite of the chocolate loaf. It was sublimely delicious.

"But then you say, 'Who am I to keep them apart,' and I have to say whoa! Slow down, Kat."

"What?"

"For starters, you're not keeping anybody apart. Nothing has happened. At least, as of now. And if it does, it does. That's basically between your mom and Orin. And from what I know of your mom, she'd never jump into anything without running it by you. But either way, you're not keeping anybody apart. You're just a person, having feelings. Lighten your load there, Voodoo Mama."

I sighed. Jac made a lot of sense.

"What, are you taking some kind of correspondence therapy course?" I asked, smiling. "Why are you so smart all of a sudden?"

"I'm only smart about other people," Jac said. "As you know, where my own mother is concerned, I'm useless. Dumb as a post. Oh man, he's here."

The last sentence stumped me.

"What? Who's here?"

Jac furiously dabbed at her lips with a

napkin, and pushed another square of choc-olate loaf in my direction, while glancing over my shoulder.

I turned around. Orin was walking to-ward our table.

"If he asks, we totally split the Rocket Loaf," Jac muttered.

I suppressed a smile. Maybe Jac was do-ing a little crushing of her own.

"Hi," Orin said.

"I thought you were going to call," I replied, and instantly regretted sounding rude. "I mean, not that you shouldn't be here — we're just dying of anticipation. Did you see Tank? Was there a difference?"

Orin pulled up a chair and sat down. He smoothed his hair back and away from his forehead.

"He's awake."

"What?" Jac and I cried simultaneously.

"Did you see him? What did he say? Did he know you? Does he remember being at the house?" I couldn't get the questions out fast enough.

"I didn't see him, or get close to him," Orin said.

"Then how —"

"I got to the hospital and went up to his floor. There was a huge commotion going on. People laughing, clapping each other on the back. Nurses hugging. Doctors going in and out of Tank's room. I've gotten to know some of the nurses, and one of them, Rita, saw me standing there. She told me that about an hour earlier Tank had spontaneously awakened. His parents were both there at the time. The doctors are running all kinds of tests on him, but at first blush he seems to have suffered no permanent damage at all. He knows who he is. He remembers the accident. He had no idea how long he'd been out."

"One hour ago . . ." I said. "Orin, that's about when we were in Tank's room."

Orin nodded, smiling broadly.

"Nice coincidence, right?"

"No! Orin, my mother says there's no such —"

"— thing as a coincidence," he finished. "And she's absolutely right."

"So did you talk to his parents?" Jac asked.

Orin sighed.

"I did," he said. "Tank's father saw me in the hallway when he was getting coffee."

"Man, he must have wanted to build you a monument!" I exclaimed. "He must have been so grateful."

Orin smiled.

"Yeah. Actually, it was pretty much the opposite."

"Why?" asked Jac.

"Tank's father was never exactly thrilled to have me doing my work. It was Tank's mom who brought me in, and he went along with it because there just weren't any other options. But he never really approved of it. So when he saw me, he got a little angry. He told me that he'd been a fool to let me mess around in his kid's room, that Tank had managed to wake up all by himself, and that I should leave the hospital because I wasn't welcome at this family reunion."

"What?" I cried. "That's outrageous! You told him that it *was* you, right? That we were doing that energy bridge at the very same moment Tank woke up! You told him that, right?"

Orin shook his head.

"But why? Why not?" I cried. It made me absolutely nuts when people got help from someone like my mom or Orin, then dumped all over them afterward, or pretended they'd never believed and that the whole thing was a joke.

"Kat, this was a hugely emotional moment for these people. Tank woke up after two years in a coma. Why it happened, and who was responsible for helping it happen, is completely irrelevant. I don't need to get credit for it. I'm not collecting case files with happy endings. Tank's awake."

"Because of you," I insisted.

"Because of us," Orin corrected.

"Right!" I retorted.

"Right," Orin agreed. "But whether or not someone else acknowledges that doesn't matter to me. I'm not a healer to pander to my ego. Healing is what I do. It's who I am. So believe me, I feel nothing but happy right now."

I was insane. I should be throwing this man at my mother, not fussing about the possibility they might become more than friends. Orin was amazing.

"So, I guess I still don't understand, Orin," I said. "If Tank was alive in the hospital, how could I see him in his house?"

"Well, I can't exactly say for sure. Nobody could. But there are people who believe that a coma is just a different form of consciousness. Similar to sleep in some ways, different in others. And I'm sure you know that many people, myself included, believe that our astral selves leave our body in the sleep state and interact with other people, both living and dead. In out-of-body experiences, the astral self leaves the body in the waking stage. It's not much of a stretch at all to believe that when someone is comatose, their astral self is roaming around outside the body.

"Tank was confused, the way many spirits are when they've died suddenly. The nature of their consciousness has changed, but they don't understand why, or how, or what the new rules of the game are. With Tank, I think his astral self began traveling more and more often, and became more and more confused.

"Eventually he returned to a place where he was comfortable — his house. But even that was different. No one lived there anymore. And nobody seemed to be able to see him. But you operate on a different frequency than most people, Kat. I think that's why Tank honed in on you. He didn't really know how to communicate. He didn't know who or what you were. But he was attracted to you like a moth to a light."

"Is he going to remember this now that he's awake?" I asked.

Orin shrugged.

"I read a book once about a doctor who was in a coma for several years, and spontaneously awakened. He had many memories of his experiences during the coma, and even recognized several of the nurses that had attended him. But his recollections sounded very dreamlike. Maybe Tank will have some recollections that seem like dreams. Or maybe it will all be a blank."

"I find it all hard to believe, and I've been wide awake the whole time," Jac remarked. She glanced over at Orin.

"Not that I *don't* believe, mind you," she added hastily. "I'm just . . . wowed."

"No, I understand," Orin said. "You've

helped, actually. You have a very bright energy." Jac flushed at the compliment.

"So what now?" I asked.

Orin looked at me.

"Well, as far as Tank goes, nothing. Happy ending, and all that. As for the house, that's entirely up to you. You know that there's someone else there who wants you to listen to him. But you're not obligated to do anything, Kat. You have a say in all this, and you know how to protect yourself now."

The old man. It all came down to him, somehow. He represented the dark side of being a medium, as did that dark shadow in the library. A spirit who was not young and sweet like Suzanne Bennis, not lost and vulnerable like Tank. An angry, ugly spirit. Helping him would not be pleasant, I knew. But if I didn't get past my fear of him, I would have to carry it inside me.

"Even if I decide to ignore that old man for now, he's still going to be there," I said. "They're all still going to be there. I've got a village following me around, and that's never going to change."

"Like the guy on the cell phone commercial, who has his network tagging along after him," Jac added helpfully.

I thought about the old man, and the other spirits in the van Hecht house. And about all those orbs, circling me like flies. I hadn't chosen them. I hadn't asked for them. But they had sought me out, and they wouldn't leave until I gave them my ear. And probably more were arriving every day.

Orin had said he could teach me to manage energetic blocks. That he could teach me other things like the energy bubble, so that I would be in control of things. I would be able to close up shop when I chose. That would make a difference. A very big difference. And that would only leave one thing for me to do — bring my fears of darker spirits under control. It wasn't a prospect I looked forward to at all. But there were people who had my back. My mom. Jac. Even Orin. It really wouldn't be such a bad thing at all to have him around more.

"Orin, do you like hummus and tahini?" I asked.

Orin nodded. Jac gave me a quizzical look.

"And pita bread? And carrot-banana smoothies?"

Orin nodded again.

"Would you like to come to my house for dinner? My mom is making all those things for tonight, and she's a pretty good cook."

Orin smiled at me in a way that made it feel like the sun had just come out.

"Kat," he said, "I'd be delighted."

"Me, too," Jac added. "I just happen to be available."

I laughed with happiness and contentment before popping the last square of chocolate loaf in my mouth.

Chapter 15

It was a nice night, all in all. It was good to have some noisy laughter around the dinner table. Even Max seemed happier than usual. And when I saw my mom enjoying herself, catching up on old times with Orin, looking so relaxed and happy and pretty, it didn't feel weird anymore to have him around. No matter what happened, or didn't happen.

Jac had spontaneously outlined her entire drama for us at the table, ending with the detail that the war at her house was continuing.

"But eventually she's going to have to realize she can't keep me under lock and key forever," Jac said.

"Jac, please tell me your mother knows where you are right now," my mom said, leaning forward with a crease of worry on her forehead.

"She does. I called her from the Bean Factory. And I called her from here when I told you I was going to the bathroom."

"So she knows you're having dinner with us," my mother pressed.

"She knows. I would not describe her as happy about it, but she agreed not to send the Marines to kick in your front door and whisk me back home. I had to promise her that we'd talk about everything when I got home, though."

"And what do you think you're going to do?" I asked. "About all of it?"

Jac moved from her chair over to the little rug by the stove that Max was curled up on. She smoothed his ears and kissed him on the nose before replying.

"It's done," Jac said. "I've quit. End of story."

"But don't you miss it at all?" I asked. "Just playing? The way it sounds, the way it feels?"

"I've quit," Jac repeated. "And maybe it isn't all good all the time. But I have my life back. Or the option of my life back. And at the end of the day, that's the most important thing. And I got that back by making the decision that I had to quit."

Max rolled onto his back and stuck his paws in the air. Jac gave him a tender smile and obligingly began to scratch his tummy.

"Out of curiosity, and understanding it's

none of my business, why exactly did you quit?" asked Orin.

We all looked at him. My mother had a tiny smile playing about her lips.

"I understand that you're giving up your mother's vision of your future. You're giving up the belief that the cello is the be-all and end-all of your daily existence. I totally get that. But does it necessarily follow that you can't ever touch the instrument again? Because giving up playing the cello as a profession doesn't mean you have to give up playing it for fun."

Jac stared at Orin, her lips pressed tightly together.

"You already know the answer, Jac," he continued. "And whatever answer you're hearing is going to be the right one for you. But just consider how you're structuring the question. You're quitting someone else's view of your gift, not the gift itself."

Jac took a sharp breath and frowned.

"Anybody else want to add their two cents?" she asked, sounding defensive.

Max extended his paws and stretched luxuriously. He made a happy little groan that ended up with something that sounded a lot like a dog burp.

Jac waited about two seconds before bursting into hysterics.

"What's so funny?" I asked. But I couldn't help laughing, too. Jac's laugh was infectious.

"All of it," Jac said. "Max. My mother. My life. I mean, it's nuts. But look at me. I'm here with my best friend, her gassy dog, and a couple of wise psychic elders who have no problem reminding me that I've got *choices*. And more important than any of that, there's *cake* for dessert!"

Orin started to laugh, too, and my mother joined in. And we laughed for a long time. We laughed until Jac interrupted us to ask if, by chance, my mother would mind if she started slicing the cake.

Chapter 16

For the remaining few days of spring break, Jac spent an enormous amount of time at our house. She somehow managed to convince her mother that they both needed some time apart. My mother spoke to her mother just long enough to confirm that Jac had been given permission, though begrudgingly, to visit me.

The previous night, we had extended the visit to a sleepover. We woke up much earlier than we meant to, and lay for a long time mulling over the events of the week. Max snored happily at the foot of my bed, but his ears twitched as we talked, like he was sleep-eavesdropping.

"It must be so nice to live here, having who you have for a mom," Jac said. "I wouldn't mind being you one bit."

"Yeah, well," I said, pulling my blanket up to my chin and curling up on my side, facing Jac in her sleeping bag. "It isn't all perfect, you know. Money is always tight. Our house is sort of falling down around our ears. My clothes were in style in the late seventies. And for all practical purposes, I don't have a dad. I worry sometimes, about how we'll get by."

"That must be scary," Jac agreed. "But seriously, wouldn't you rather have no money, and be really happy at home? I mean, your mom is practically perfect."

I laughed.

"Practically perfect according to whom? She's a medium. She contacts the dead for a very minimal fee. She drives a fifteen-year-old car. She walks the dog barefoot. I don't think everyone would be in agreement that she's 'perfect.'"

"She's perfect for you," Jac said. "You're perfect for each other."

"Probably," I replied. "But sometimes that's an issue, too. I don't know. Sometimes I just feel like I need to start being more independent. It doesn't have anything to do with her personally.

"It's just, I don't know. Ever since I turned thirteen, I've felt like I had to kind of establish a little space between us. I need to be me by myself — not attached to her all the time. She'll help me through everything. Regular stuff and supernatural stuff. And for some reason I just feel like I have to not let her. Does that make any sense?"

"Maybe a tiny bit," Jac said. "But I'd still rather be you any day of the week."

"You've got a better nose," I said.

"You've got better hair," Jac countered.

"Your butt is smaller," I stated.

"You're taller," she shot back.

"You've got cuter feet," I declared.

Jac grinned.

"Well now, that is true. I *do* have cuter feet."

We laughed, and I threw one of my pillows at Jac's head.

"I can't believe we have to go back to school on Monday," Jac said, throwing the pillow back at me. Max opened one eye, then closed it again.

"I know," I said. "And we need to finish the basic communications project today," I reminded Jac.

"You got the pages I e-mailed you, right?" Jac asked.

"Yeah. They're really good. But we have to get the whole thing into a finished form. Choose which pictures to use. Lay out the text and pictures. Print it."

"That'll only take an hour," Jac said, snuggling under her blanket.

"Maybe two," I said.

"We'll do it this afternoon. First, let's do something fun," Jac said. "Let's take the bus into town. We can go shopping."

"I can't afford to go shopping," I said.

"Well, you can afford to take the bus," Jac replied. "Let's go into town and have some fun."

I agreed. We dressed quickly, stopping for a quick detour in the kitchen.

"No one bakes like this," Jac said, her mouth full of blueberry muffin. "Your mom could make a fortune if she ever opened a bakery. Remind me to kiss her feet the next time I see her. Is she still asleep?"

"She's probably meditating," I said. "She does that for an hour every morning."

Jac said something I couldn't make out, because she'd taken another large bite.

"Can we go already?" I urged her.

Jac nodded, and we left the kitchen and headed out the front door. On the sidewalk, I stopped by the van Hecht's mailbox and put something inside it.

"What was that?" Jac asked.

"Something I found in the backyard," I explained. "A little toy tank. I'm guessing it belonged to our Tank. Seems like it ought to stay with the house."

We stood for a moment, looking up at the peeling clapboards.

"It is a nice house," Jac said, and I nodded.

We were turning to go when we saw a car slow down and turn into the van Hechts' driveway. A man got out of the driver's seat and opened the back door. He helped someone else get out of the back of the car. The man caught sight of me and Jac and waved hello. When we waved back, he walked over to us.

"'Morning," he said.

"Hi," I replied. "I'm Kat. I live right here," I told him, pointing at our house.

"Ah, good!" he said. "I'm Marcus van Hecht. I own this house. We moved away a few years back and were going to sell the place, but we're thinking about moving back in now."

Someone walked up behind Mr. van Hecht, and the man turned and put his arm around the boy.

"And this is my son, Tank," he said, grinning broadly.

I took a sharp breath, and felt fortunate that I hadn't accidentally blurted out a shocked sound.

"Hi," I said, trying to sound casual. "I'm Kat, and this is Jac."

"Hey," Tank said. "Nice to meet you."

He was taller than I thought he'd be. He looked exactly my age now, no longer the skinny boy I'd seen upstairs. He was a bit frail, and leaned on a cane for support. His face was quite handsome, though there was something funny about his eyes. He had the slightly confused look of someone who'd just woken up abruptly, which I supposed, in a way, he had.

"Well, hopefully we'll see you around," Mr. van Hecht said. "My wife will be coming by later. She was worried the house would be nothing but a heap, imagining people were vandalizing it and breaking in every day."

"Oh, we don't have many break-ins around here," I said, feeling guilty. I was probably the only culprit.

"Yes, of course. Excellent," Mr. van Hecht said. I tried to return his smile, but it was hard. I couldn't help remembering how he'd dismissed Orin. I still felt kind of mad about it.

We said our good-byes, and I started to turn away when Tank spoke.

"I . . . do we know each other?" Tank asked. "I mean, have we met before today?"

It was hard to meet Tank's gaze, but I made myself do it.

"You just seem sort of familiar," Tank added, because I hadn't responded. "When did you move here?"

"Two years ago," I said, and Tank wrinkled his forehead.

"Oh," he said. "Well then I wouldn't . . . I guess we couldn't have met, then."

"Oh, I don't know," I said. "It's a strange world. Anything is possible."

Tank gave me a funny look, then nodded and waved a good-bye.

It certainly was a strange world. But I wasn't terrified of what was in mine anymore. The butterflies in my stomach had gone.

Tomorrow, I had my first lesson scheduled with Orin, and I had already decided what I'd do afterward. I would go to the van Hechts' house and break in for the last time. I would face the old man, not because he was scaring me into it, but because I was choosing to help him. After that, I wouldn't be a Scaredy Kat anymore.

I had no doubt that there would be new things that would frighten me. But, with help, there was nothing supernatural I couldn't handle. I would always see dead people. But now it would be on my terms, not theirs.

It was a strange world. I'd met a ghost, and soon he'd be moving in next door.

If that could happen, then anything was possible.

FICTION

6/09